ALL I'VE EVER WANTED

A strange, yet familiar yearning fluttered in the pit of her stomach and a sudden haze clouded her head. She frowned, uncertain whether it was the beer or the intriguing man that affected her in such a way.

"You want another one?" Maxwell asked.

Kennedy looked up, confused. "What?"

"Drink." He pointed to her empty bottle. "You want another drink?"

She blinked. When had she finished it? "Sure."

Max got up and went into the kitchen. As he walked away, she took her time assessing him. His gait was confident and graceful—and he didn't have a bad butt, either. She looked at his shoulders and remembered their comfort. It was then that Kennedy realized she could fall in love with Detective Maxwell Collier.

BOOK YOUR PLACE ON OUR WEBSITE AND MAKE THE ARABESQUE ROMANCE CONNECTION!

We've created a customized website just for our very special Arabesque readers, where you can get the inside scoop on everything that's going on with Arabesque romance novels.

When you come online, you'll have the exciting opportunity to:

- View covers of upcoming books

- Learn about our future publishing schedule (listed by publication month and author)

- Find out when your favorite authors will be visiting a city near you

- Search for and order backlist books

- Check out author bios and background information

- Send e-mail to your favorite authors

- Join us in weekly chats with authors, readers and other guests

- Get writing guidelines

- AND MUCH MORE!

Visit our website at
http://www.arabesquebooks.com

ALL I'VE EVER WANTED

Adrianne Byrd

ARABESQUE
★BET.
BOOKS

BET Publications, LLC
www.bet.com
www.arabesquebooks.com

ARABESQUE BOOKS are published by

BET Publications, LLC
c/o BET BOOKS
One BET Plaza
1900 W Place NE
Washington, D.C. 20018-1211

All Kensington Titles, Imprints, and Distributed Lines are avail-
able at special quantity discounts for bulk purchases for sales
promotions, premiums, fund-raising, and educational or insti-
tutional use. Special book excerpts or customized printings can
also be created to fit specific needs. For details, write or phone
the office of the Kensington special sales manager: Kensington
Publishing Corp., 850 Third Avenue, New York, NY 10022,
attn: Special Sales Department, Phone: 1-800-221-2647.

First Printing: May 2001
10 9 8 7 6 5 4 3 2 1

Printed in the United States of America

One

Exhausted, Kennedy St. James stared out the city bus window and into the night. Her vision never focused on anything in particular as she allowed her mind to wander endlessly on everything and nothing. She shifted in her seat and once again felt the painful throb in her feet. Lord, how she hated waiting tables.

She pulled her gaze from the passing trees and looked around the MARTA bus just as Mrs. Russell pulled the thin, wired cord above her head. A bell dinged and the elderly woman rose from her seat. Their eyes met seconds before they shared a smile.

"You have a nice night," Mrs. Russell said kindly before shuffling down the narrow aisle.

"You, too," Kennedy responded. She watched as the woman exchanged pleasantries with Leroy, the bus driver, then stepped off the bus.

"God bless that sweet woman," Leroy said, shaking his head as he pulled the bus away from the curb. He looked up into his rearview mirror and locked gazes with Kennedy. "I've never met anyone with such a kind spirit. You know what I mean?"

She nodded and smiled. "I know exactly what you mean."

"Why God saw it fit to take her husband, then turn around and take both her children in the same year just escapes me."

Kennedy remembered her father's funeral and absently quoted what her grandmother had told her. "Some things aren't for us to understand."

"I suppose you're right," he agreed, nodding. "It just breaks my heart to see her in such bad shape."

The subtle smile curved across Kennedy's face suddenly felt heavy and forced. In fact, lately all her smiles seemed that way. Her grandmother once said that life should be viewed like a roller coaster ride. Everyone has a share of ups and downs. But, for years now, Kennedy's life seemed like one fast dip into oblivion. When was her ride going to climb back up?

The slow, gentle rocking of the MARTA bus as it traveled down Martin Luther King Boulevard reminded her of her grandmother's old rocking chair, which had lulled her into more than her fair share of catnaps. She glanced at her watch. It wouldn't be long before she could climb into bed to get as close to eight hours of sleep as she possibly could—which would probably be her usual four hours.

Working long hours, plus attending night school, was definitely taking its toll. The sad fact was that she still had a good two years to go before she received her bachelor's degree. She expelled a long sigh. Did she really have what it would take to get through another two years?

She would be nearly thirty years old by the time she finished. But it was better to be thirty with a degree, than to be that age without one, she reminded herself. Had she not started her family young, she would have been finished with school by now. "Better late than never," she reaffirmed softly.

When her stop came into view, she pulled the cord, and then stood to slip her bookbag across her shoulders.

"You have a good weekend, Leroy," she said, offering another heavy smile.

The older man's dark eyes twinkled as his lips widened. "You do the same, Kennedy. But make sure you get yourself some rest. You look like you're about to pass out."

The doors jerked open.

"Trust me. The moment my head hits the pillow it's lights out. But I'll see you Monday night." She waved and then stepped off the bus.

The engine roared as the bus pulled away from the curb and off. The night's cool breeze picked up velocity and the trees lining the walkway rustled in protest.

Kennedy glanced around the deserted street, accustomed to its eerie feel. Zipping up her faded denim jacket, she hoped that she wouldn't turn into a Popsicle by the time she made it home.

She noted a pack of stray dogs patrolling the area and watched in amazement as they actually waited until the traffic light changed before crossing. Kennedy shook her head and picked up her pace. With each step, her feet throbbed harder, but she'd promised Eve that she'd make it home no later than a quarter after. The last thing she needed was to lose another babysitter.

From the corner of her eye, she spotted a small break in a row of bushes and remembered a shortcut through the woods. That way, she would make it home with a few minutes to spare. Impulsively, she took the shortcut.

A bed of leaves crinkled beneath her feet as she marched onward. The lights from the road disappeared as she moved through a thicket of trees. Strange noises surrounded her and fear slowed her footsteps.

With only a sliver of moonlight to guide her, and an accelerated heartbeat distracting her, she paused, suddenly unsure that she was headed in the right direction. Kennedy squinted at the worn trail. Yes, she was going the right way.

Harsh sounds disturbed her and raised the tiny hairs on the back of her neck. She stopped again and tried to listen. It was hard at first, but then it became clear that what she was hearing wasn't animals or birds, but voices—angry voices.

She thought about turning around, but only briefly. Her curiosity, which had often been her undoing, rose and urged her onward, like a red flag in front of a bull's nose. It wouldn't hurt to go and check it out. She'd often heard that the local teenagers sneaked out here to do God knows what, with God knows whom. Wanda, her best friend, suspected that her thirteen-year-old son came out here to drink with the older teenagers.

"He better not be," Kennedy mumbled under her breath as she turned toward the voices.

Two

Four-year-old Thomas St. James's eyes flew open. Disoriented, he stared into the black void that enveloped him. Why had he insisted that he didn't need his nightlight? Big boys don't use nightlights, he reminded himself. Of course he didn't know whether he really believed that. But since his best friend, Jimmy, said it, then it must be true.

Tommy swallowed his fear and threw back the covers. If he ran to the door, then maybe the monster under the bed wouldn't catch him. He shook his head. Mommy said there were no such things as monsters. He frowned, he wasn't too sure that he believed that either.

He climbed out of bed and, the minute his feet touched the floor, sprinted across the room. When he pulled the door open, lights flickering from the television sprayed funny pictures across the walls of the hallway. He knew immediately that his mother hadn't made it home.

Disappointment creased his brows and his shoulders slumped. Slowly, he headed toward the living room to see if Eve was still awake. She had only been babysitting him for a week, but he'd already made up his mind that he liked her. He'd never met a girl before who loved baseball and chocolate pudding as much as he did.

"Eve?" he called when he didn't immediately see her.

Almost instantly he saw her head pop up above the back of the sofa as she sat up and turned around to face him. "Tommy," she said, rubbing her eyes. She glanced at her watch. "What are you doing up? Is something wrong?" She jumped to her feet and rushed toward him.

He blushed when she gathered him close and kissed his brow.

"Did you have a bad dream?"

He shook his head. "Where's Mommy?"

Eve frowned as she looked at her watch. "I don't know, but I'm sure she'll be home soon. Do you want me to read you another bedtime story?"

He considered it for a moment, and then shook his head. "Can I wait up for her with you? I don't have to go to school tomorrow. I'm sure she won't mind."

"I don't know. A growing boy needs his sleep."

"Please? I'll be quiet and stay out of your way."

"Sweetheart, you don't have to make such promises. I don't mind if you wait up with me. Now, you're sure your mother won't mind?"

He nodded eagerly.

"Well, all right then." She offered him her hand, and then led him to the sofa.

He helped clear her books away, then bounced up to sit next to her. She smelled like flowers. "I wish that you will always be my babysitter," he gushed.

"Oh really?" She smiled. "Why is that?"

He shrugged and blushed again. "Because you're nice."

"Aw. That's sweet." She pinched his cheek. "I think you're nice, too."

They shared another smile before she looked at her watch again.

"I wonder what's keeping your mother?"

Kennedy had made a terrible mistake.

No sooner had she rounded a giant oak tree than her incredulous stare focused on a horrific scene—not Wanda's wayward son, but four men clothed in black, with cross-bones stitched across their jackets. The men stood menacingly around an impeccably-clad, older man with nervous eyes. From what she could see, he had every right to be nervous.

She glanced around, wanting desperately to retrace her steps and forget that she'd seen anything. However, there was one problem with that plan. Her feet seemed rooted to the ground. She prayed, yet no sooner had she whispered the Lord's name than she caught a glimpse of a gun.

Instinctively, she ducked back behind the tree, surprised that she'd managed to move at all. *Run.* But she couldn't. Instead, she closed her eyes and tried to calm down. When she reopened her eyes, she could still hear the men arguing.

She pushed away from the tree, then hesitated to take the first step. There were dry leaves everywhere. Surely, if she made any attempt to get away, she would draw attention to herself. The mere fact that they hadn't heard her approach was a miracle.

She squeezed her eyes shut and prayed again. The

men's angry voices shattered the woods' stillness. Her heartbeat accelerated. Despite her decision not to get involved, Kennedy found herself listening.

"Tell your boss I was coming to talk to him."

Kennedy assumed the new voice belonged to the well-dressed businessman. Despite his efforts to sound aloof, or to retain some type of control, she heard fear in his voice. She absorbed his emotions as her own.

"You're not listening, old man. Now, turn around."

Kennedy's eyes flew open. She knew that voice. Carefully, she shifted her weight and peeked around the tree, squinting for a better view of the armed man. Her heart sank as she confirmed the man's identity. Then, slowly, her gaze drifted to the businessman.

The moonlight illuminated the tears streaking down his face. He knew as well as she did that they were going to kill him.

"I said turn around!"

"Just call your boss," he pleaded. "I swear I can clear this whole mess up." Desperation made the man's voice quake.

Another member of the gang physically forced the man to turn around.

Fear squeezed Kennedy's heart. She had to do something, but what—scream? Hell, that would just mean there would be two corpses instead of one. It wasn't like she could attack with her bookbag and actually hope to save the day.

"Please, I swear I can clear this all up." The man continued to plead. His entire body trembled.

Kennedy quaked with an overwhelming sense of helplessness as tears blurred her vision.

The man was forced to his knees and all residue

of pride vanished. Words spilled from his lips, but none of them made any sense.

Dear God, no. Kennedy whispered silently.

The gun was placed at the back of the sobbing man's head. Still, she hoped for a miracle.

A single shot ended it all.

The man's body pitched forward, finally falling into a bed of dry leaves.

Kennedy jumped, but managed to suppress a horrified scream by clamping her hand over her mouth. Tears slid quietly down her face. She felt numb as she desperately tried to deny what she'd witnessed.

"No," she whispered, backing away from the tree. When she moved, the leaves beneath her feet crackled at an alarming volume.

"What the hell was that?"

Kennedy's head rang with the horrifying realization of what she'd just done.

"Mike and Devon, go check it out."

Her thoughts scrambled. *They're going to kill me.* The realization thawed the fear and self-preservation kicked into high gear.

She turned and ran.

"Over there," she heard a man yell a split second before something whizzed by her ear.

Don't stop. Don't stop. Dodging around trees, jumping over bushes and rocks, Kennedy ran as fast as she could. Branches snapped and she kicked up dirt and leaves as she passed. The men were still shooting. She thought of her son and ran faster, fearing she would never see him again.

Three

Detective Maxwell Collier groaned inwardly as he parked his black Maxima behind a swarm of patrol cars. The sun had barely been up for an hour and it was already time to deal with the aftermath of a full moon. Dread seeped into his bones as he stared at the dismal scene from behind his dark sunglasses.

A quick tap against his window drew him out of his trance. When he looked up, he saw his partner, Det. Michael Dossman, grinning crookedly and holding two steaming cups of coffee. Whether Max liked it or not, it was time to face the day.

"Morning," Dossman greeted, handing Max a cup as he got out of his car. "I hope you enjoyed your vacation because we've just been handed a case from hell."

Max groaned. One could hardly call spending a week on an ugly custody battle a vacation. "After fifteen years on the force, I've come to the conclusion that every case is a case from hell."

Dossman shrugged. "I guess you have a point there.

But this is one for the record books," he said as they headed toward the crime scene.

"Just spit it out, Dossman."

"I think I'd rather wait until you see it for yourself."

"Suit yourself." Max shrugged off his irritation at his partner's baiting game and took a sip of his coffee. Now the morning was complete.

He didn't know what he'd expected, if he'd expected anything at all, but he'd recognized the victim. In one glance, he realized the truth of Dossman's statement; this *was* going to be the case from hell. "Assistant District Attorney, Marion Underwood."

"I see you have a good memory," Dossman said. "Frankly, I never cared for the man."

"That goes for everyone who ever met him." Max exhaled, and then took a look around the perimeter. "What in the hell was he doing out here?"

"Now that's the million dollar question."

"This definitely wasn't a robbery gone awry."

"No. This looks more like an execution: a single bullet to the back of the head. It doesn't look like anything was taken. The man still had twenty-five hundred dollars in cash and six platinum cards in his wallet."

"Who discovered the body?" Max questioned.

"A group of teenagers. They said this place is a popular make out point. Can you believe that?"

"Here? It's the middle of nowhere."

Dossman smiled. "They say that that's the beauty of it."

"Of course. What was I thinking?" Suddenly, his coffee lost its appeal. "The media is going to have a field day with this one."

"There's that. There's also the fact that we have no leads and no witnesses."

"And no suspects."

Dossman shook his head. "On the contrary. I suspect that we'll be swimming in suspects. It'll be a 'Who shot J.R.' kind of thing."

"Great. I can hardly wait. How much time do you think we have before—"

"Detective Collier, Detective Collier. May I ask you a few questions?"

Max jerked around to Aaliyah Hunter. She was clutching a microphone and her cameraman was waving frantically. The sight of them twisted his stomach into knots.

"She's got to be kidding," Dossman said, shaking his head. "Wasn't she the reporter who put you in the hot seat last year?"

"Hot seat?" Max ground his teeth, then turned away. "She damn near cost me my job with her misquotes and creative editing skills." To his surprise, his face flushed with anger. He'd thought that he'd turned the corner long ago and put the whole incident behind him.

"I can see why you were easily led down the road to hell." Dossman openly assessed the reporter's physical assets. "A woman who looks like that could only be trouble."

Max cast another glance at Ms. Hunter. He hated to admit that his partner had a point. She *was* perfect; too perfect. With her long hair, her dancer's legs, and her Colgate smile, she definitely spelled trouble. "Do me a favor?" Max said, returning his attention to Dossman. "Stay clear of her."

"That could have gone without saying. Let me be the first to remind you to do the same."

For the first time that morning, Max allowed a smile to curve his lips. "Consider it done."

"Detective Collier," another female voice rang out.

He turned toward his fellow detective, Julia Washington, who was waving him over. "I think you better take a look at this."

"You go ahead," Dossman encouraged. "I'm going to see if I can work out who was the last person to see Mr. Underwood alive. Maybe I'll get lucky and find his datebook. I should be able to search his office or place of residence. Let's say we check in with each other"— he glanced at his watch—"in about three hours. Is that good with you?"

"Sounds like a plan." Max nodded, then headed toward Detective Washington. As he walked he took a closer look at his surroundings. What an odd place for teenagers to hang out. Back in his day, if he'd even thought about bringing a girl to some remote area like this, he'd never have even gotten near first base. Surely women hadn't changed so much that they no longer wanted to be romanced or wooed.

"What did you find, Julia?"

"Casings. Several of them, in fact. If I was a betting woman, I'd say they are from more than one gun."

He frowned. "I thought that our victim was killed execution style?"

"He was. But I'd say that whoever killed him wasn't alone and perhaps Underwood wasn't intended to be the only victim."

Kennedy flinched as she removed the small Band-Aid from her ear. At least it had stopped bleeding, she consoled. She leaned toward the mirror to get a better look and grimaced when she fingered her left lobe. She would probably never be able to wear earrings in that ear again.

She opened the medicine cabinet and found a half-empty bottle of peroxide. She tended her discolored ear as best she could, then placed another Band-aid over the wound.

Slowly, she moved away from the vanity area and over to the tub, where she turned the shower on and made the water as hot as she could stand it. As she disrobed, she gazed at the numerous scratches that marred her skin. How she had survived that horrible night was beyond her. All she could remember was running. . . .

"This way," a man yelled to his companions.

He was a little too close for comfort. The thought of giving up crossed her mind, but she quickly dispelled the notion. She'd never considered herself a quitter and she had no intention of becoming one now.

Her lungs burned and her legs ached as she finally broke through into the clearing around her development. She wasted no time gauging her location; she ducked into the first building she reached. She knew the building's floor plan well since it was a duplicate of her own.

Keep moving, keep moving. *Down the stairs and into the basement, she ran.* Faster, faster, *she urged herself. When her hands pushed opened the laundry room door, she heard a crash on the floor above her. Her heart pounded as she plunged onward.*

She stopped short the moment she spotted the small window. There were shards of broken glass scattered everywhere beneath it and two wooden boards were nailed across the opening. Dear God, what am I going to do now? . . .

"Mommy, can Jimmy go to church with us this morning?" Tommy's inquisitive voice broke Kennedy's reverie and jerked her back to the present.

"Uh . . . Sure, Honey. As long as it's okay with his mother," she answered above the sound of the shower spray. She couldn't remember when she'd stepped into the shower, or even lathering, but she rushed to rinse off. She had a million and one things to do before they left for the eleven o'clock service.

Determined to put Friday night's events behind her, Kennedy concentrated on preparing breakfast, which consisted of milk and cereal due to her running behind schedule. As usual, Jimmy's mother had dropped him off without feeding him breakfast and Kennedy found herself preparing another bowl.

While the boys ate, Kennedy mended her son's only good pair of slacks and then rushed to get dressed herself. By ten o'clock, she had everyone clothed, fed, and standing at the bus stop.

"Mommy, are you okay?" Tommy questioned, swinging her hand.

Startled, she jumped and refocused her attention on her son. "Of course, baby. Mommy is just thinking that's all." Her forced smile grew warm as she stared down at him. Every time she saw him she was reminded of how much he looked like his father.

Standing beside Tommy was Jimmy. He was only six months older than her son, but probably weighed a good twenty pounds more. He had the deepest pair of dimples she had ever seen, and right now the boy also had the misfortune to be missing his two front teeth. It was impossible not to like the exuberant boy. In fact, she often felt more like a second mother to him than a neighbor.

Their bus arrived and the three of them stepped on and took their seats. Throughout the ride, Kennedy remained on guard. Of course, she still had no idea what she'd do if she recognized one of the gang members from the other night.

Just put the whole thing behind you, she coached herself. But, even as she thought the words, her thoughts traveled back to that night . . .

"He had to have gone this way," the now familiar voice shouted.

As what sounded like a stampede descended the stairs, again Kennedy felt as if her feet had rooted themselves to the floor. She couldn't seem to think. Couldn't move. Then her eyes fell on the double-load dryers and a solution became clear.

Now she could move again. She ducked inside one of the dryers in a time an Olympic sprinter would envy, and tossed strange clothes over her body. Just as she finished and pulled the dryer door closed from the inside, she heard the laundry room door burst open.

She heard sounds, for a while, then everything went quiet.

Were they still in the room? Were they searching the other dryers? The possibility terrified her. She closed her eyes and prayed. Hard.

Time stretched. Yet, she still couldn't hear anything. Should she risk a peek? Her heart lurched. How had she gotten herself into this mess? The answer came quickly: her damn curiosity.

Lord, if you'll get me out of this one, I swear I'll mind my own business from now on. *Hadn't she promised that before?* I mean it this time, *she added.*

Even after her pledge, Kennedy remained in the dryer for some time. She couldn't be sure whether her prayer had been answered, but she couldn't stay cramped in there forever. Shifting her weight, she started to push open the door, just as it jerked open from the other side.

A woman screamed before she could.

"I'm sorry. I'm sorry," Kennedy apologized as she climbed out.

The other woman turned out to be a teenager, and the sheer horror etched in her features would have been comical under different circumstances. This time, Kennedy thought it would be best not to offer an explanation. She simply handed the woman the laundry that was still draped over her and took off.

By the time she made it home, it was well after one in the morning. To her surprise and relief, Eve accepted her excuse of having missed the bus and having had to catch a ride with a colleague. . . .

"Mommy, isn't this our stop?" Tommy asked.

Kennedy jumped again, but quickly got her bearings. "Yes, sweetie. Go ahead and pull the cord. Jimmy, are you ready?"

His two dimples appeared as he nodded and Kennedy had to resist the urge to pinch his chubby cheeks. Despite his cheerful presence, she was as jumpy as a preteen at a horror movie. She had to keep telling herself there was nothing to worry about. No one had seen her that night. She might as well relax.

She held hands with both boys and led them down the aisle. But, as she hurried, her purse strap snagged on something and jerked her back. She turned to pry the straps loose, but stopped cold when her gaze met a murderer's.

Four

Aaliyah Hunter clenched her teeth while her anger simmered. She knew damn well that Det. Collier had heard her asking him for an interview. She didn't have much time before other members of the press arrived on the scene. She'd already tried talking to the other members of the police force on the scene, and they'd all told her that they weren't able to comment at this time. That was a lot of crap.

"I have to figure out some way to get an exclusive."

"Good luck," Reggie Weiss, her cameraman, said from behind her. "It seems that everyone is avoiding us like the plague."

She turned and flashed him an irritated glare. "I'm quite aware of that. Thank you."

Reggie shrugged. "Forgive me for stating the obvious."

Aaliyah returned her attention to the crime scene, and particularly to Det. Collier. Maybe she should have thought twice before crossing him. She shook her head to dispel any thoughts of wrongdoing on her part. Hell, she'd just been doing her job. Why couldn't people understand that?

A cool breeze ruffled her hair and sent chills down

her spine. She cursed. There had to be something she could do here other than freezing her butt off.

"You know, there's always the possibility that they really don't have any information," Reggie offered. "I'd say, judging by your friend's expression, that he doesn't know what the hell happened out here."

"Great. Are you suggesting that we now do our investigative reports by reading body language?"

"Hey, there's no reason to take my head off. I'm not the one who burned the bridges."

He was right, she realized. Her gaze locked on Collier. He was a fine specimen of a man. At six foot two, he had a body of a pro athlete, and a face of a movie star. What red-blooded woman wouldn't be attracted to him? Even now, as she stared at him, she could feel her pulse quickening. In truth, when she'd made the decision to reedit her exclusive interview with him six months ago, it had been a direct result of a lovers' quarrel—for him, a one night stand.

A slow smile curved her lips. It hadn't been easy to seduce the dedicated detective, but the reward had been well worth the work. He'd surprised her by being a tender and sensual lover. So much so, that she still dreamed of that night. So much so, that she'd vowed to have him again.

Kennedy's heart stopped, or at least it felt that way. She stared at the man she'd seen in the woods, Keenan Lawrence, the leader of The Skulls. She couldn't believe that she'd run into him here of all places.

"Mommy, come on," Tommy called, tugging on her arm.

Wordlessly, she pried her purse strap loose from the

bus seat, and then managed to turn away from the gang member's black glare. She could feel his gaze burning through her, as she somehow managed to get the children off the bus. Only then was she able to heave a sigh of relief.

However, that relief didn't last long. Throughout the church service, Kennedy badgered herself over the way she'd behaved on the bus. If Keenan hadn't suspected her before, she'd just given him a reason to. She shook her head and vowed to do better if their paths crossed again.

Maybe I should call the police. Kennedy almost laughed aloud at the thought. To go to the police would be like signing her own death warrant. She looked down at Tommy and realized that she had a lot more than just her own life at stake. She knew the streets well enough to know that The Skulls were a force to be reckoned with and no amount of police protection could protect you from the infamous gang.

When it came time for every head to bow, she prayed for forgiveness, guidance, and above all wisdom. Cowardice was a bitter pill to swallow, she realized.

After the service, Pastor Warner approached Kennedy. "Ms. St. James, I'm glad to see you. The missus and I wanted to thank you for helping with the children's Bible study last week. I swear I don't know where you find the time to help out with the church's functions, but I'm mighty glad that you do."

She offered him a genuine smile. "There's no need to thank me. I'm glad that I was able to help. Really."

"I see that you brought Mr. Hughes with you again," he said, referring to little Jimmy. "You know our church is always happy to see more young black men enter the Lord's house."

Jimmy grinned broadly, displaying the gap in his front teeth.

Kennedy had discovered long ago that he loved it when he was referred to as Mr. Hughes. Especially since his mother always called him "the man of the house." She placed a comforting arm around Jimmy's shoulders as well as Tommy's.

"Well, we all enjoyed your sermon this morning."

"Good. Does that mean you'll be returning this evening for the six o'clock revival?"

"I wish we could, but—"

He held up his hand to cut her off. "Don't worry, I understand." His smile widened to reflect his sincerity. "You know, you've been a member of this church since—what, you were three?"

She nodded.

"I know that you've traveled a hard road. And you may have even harder times ahead of you. I just want you to know that I think that you're doing a wonderful job, caring for Tommy and putting yourself through school. I know both of your parents are proud and smiling down at you right now."

Tears welled in Kennedy's eyes. "Thank you," she managed to say, but her voice cracked under the emotional strain. In truth, she often wondered if she'd still be a great disappointment to her parents. Her highly educated parents had certainly been quite vocal about how she was throwing her life away, when they'd heard that she was pregnant.

Somehow, she succeeded in saying her goodbyes while her mind whirled over her pastor's praises. She'd give anything to hear her father say that she was doing a good job, or even have her mother around to give her advice on pediatric care. Lord knew she could have used some when Tommy was a baby.

She smiled at the memories those thoughts evoked. As a teenager, Kennedy hadn't been a rebel, nor was she "the girl next door" type. She'd considered herself to be in the middle. Ordinary. Which was exactly what she hadn't wanted to be. The funny thing was that she couldn't see how to change that, until she ran into Lee Carsey. Her smile widened.

Lee was an ordinary girl's dream. He was the captain of the football, basketball, and swim teams. Kennedy had often thought that when Lee smiled, he could light up the darkest room, no matter how cliché that sounded. The mere fact that he'd even noticed her proved that God indeed answered prayers.

When she was on Lee's s arm, suddenly, the other students had taken notice. She hadn't been so ordinary anymore.

She's thought it was the romance of the century—a love of a lifetime. They'd done everything and gone everywhere together. There were times where she hadn't been sure where he began and she ended. She'd been engaged and four months pregnant when she lost her lover in a horrible motorcycle accident. She missed and longed for him.

Kennedy withdrew from her private thoughts long enough to take the boys to Piccadilly's Cafeteria. The restaurant had long been a part of their Sunday ritual. It was also a place where she could continue to mingle with the church crowd, though her heart wasn't in such socializing today. She'd rather spend the rest of the day watching Tommy and Jimmy tell jokes over flavored Jell-O.

As the boys played, she reveled in their youth and carefree ways. Soon, she jumped into their joke-telling, and even made fun of the latest street slang terms. Why couldn't every day be Sunday? she wondered.

By three o'clock, the threesome piled back on MARTA and headed home. For Kennedy, the day's nostalgic peace had ended and her fears returned. No matter how hard she tried to act normally, she couldn't help casting worried glances over her shoulders.

Max felt the stirrings of a migraine. Nothing about this scene made any sense. That wasn't exactly unusual for a murder case, but he'd hoped for a nice simple scenario and a quick resolution that would appease his boss, and the media as well.

His cell phone rang.

"Yeah."

"Hey, partner. Any new news?" Dossman's inquisitive voice filtered through the line.

"Not yet. What about you? How are things coming?"

"I'm waiting for a judge to sign a warrant to let us search Underwood's home for his datebooks, calendars and memorandums. There's no one there who can give us a consent to search. That's why I called. What do you say you meet me at Underwood's residence around five o'clock? I should have this taken care of by then."

Max jotted the address down in his notebook and agreed to meet Dossman. He hung up just as Detective Washington returned, shaking her head.

"Well, there's definitely no shortage of footprints out here. Being that this is supposedly a popular place with the local kids, we could spend a lot of time following tracks and still end up following the wrong trail."

Max removed his shades and sighed with frustration. "The evidence still needs to be cataloged, too. That might lead us to the right trail. By the way, how many casings did we find?"

"Twenty-five, so far."

"It looks like you were right. They were chasing something."

"Or someone."

Max remained silent for a moment, then said, "Maybe someone stumbled on the scene."

"A teenager," Washington suggested.

"That would be my first guess. And since we haven't found a second body, I'm willing to bet that we've got ourselves a witness out there somewhere."

Five

Max parked his car behind Dossman's Buick and took a quick glance at his watch. Five-fifteen. He wasn't too late. He climbed out of his car and stared up at Underwood's impressive three-story home. "I knew I should have gone to law school," he mumbled sarcastically under his breath.

Slowly, he pivoted on his heel and took in the long spiraling driveway, the lush landscape, and the idyllic location. "Nice."

When he heard the front door open, he turned and locked gazes with his partner. "Can you believe this place?"

"Wait until you see the inside," Dossman said.

Max shook his head and followed his partner inside. His brows rose with suspicion at the home's picturesque decor. "You've got to be kidding me?"

"Wish I was."

"Exactly how much does an ADA make?"

"You tell me and then we'll both know." Dossman shrugged. "This has to be the cleanest place I've ever been in. I'm almost afraid to touch anything."

"Was anyone here when you arrived?"

"Yeah, the ex-wife."

"Judge Hickman is here?" Max asked, surprised.

"Believe it or not she lives here."

"Where is she now?"

Dossman tilted his head toward the ceiling. "She's upstairs crying her eyes out."

He didn't believe it. "I was under the impression that she hated Marion's guts."

"Well, she did marry the man three times. He must have been doing something right."

"They'd also divorced three times."

"According to Judge Hickman, they'd reconciled their differences and were engaged to be married again next month."

Max lifted his brows in incredulity.

Dossman shrugged. "What can I say? If at first you don't succeed . . ."

Just then their attention was drawn to the sound of footsteps overhead. Seconds later, Judge Sandra Hickman descended the staircase.

Sandra, a handsome, statuesque woman with kind eyes, met the men's gazes and lifted her chin. A veteran of her courtroom, Max had difficulty believing that the subdued woman standing before him was the same tyrannical judge who would hold a person in contempt for having looked at her the wrong way.

"Good evening, Detective Collier." She smiled politely, and wiped at her tear-reddened eyes.

He nodded in acknowledgement. "Judge."

"Can I get you gentlemen anything from the kitchen?"

"No ma'am," the men answered in unison.

Her smile wavered briefly. She turned, and stopped. "Is there anything I can do to help you with your investigation?"

Max didn't know what to make of this gentler Judge

Hickman. He'd fully expected to have to fight her for the smallest piece of information.

He decided not to look a gift horse in the mouth. "If you have a few minutes, I would like to ask you a few questions."

"Of course. Why don't you two join me in the kitchen for some tea."

Max glanced at his partner and saw the surprise on his face.

"Go ahead," Dossman encouraged. "I need to make a phone call. Mind if I use the phone?"

"Not at all. There's a phone in the den," she answered.

Max nodded and said, "Call me if you find anything," then followed Hickman.

As they walked down the long hallway, Max continued to be impressed by the lavishly appointed home.

"This is a beautiful home," he said as they entered the kitchen.

"Thank you." She gestured toward a table. "Won't you have a seat?"

Suddenly, Max suspected that the tables had been turned and that he was the one about to be interrogated. He suppressed a smile at having been sucked in by the judge's demure act.

"Detective Dossman informs me that you are the lead detective on my husband's case."

Good old Dossman passing the buck. "I understood that you and Mr. Underwood were estranged."

"Only on paper," she said.

Who was he to question her claim of true love? It wasn't like *he* knew the secrets to a successful marriage. But marrying the *same* person three times . . . ?

He took out his notepad. "Did your husband have any enemies?"

"Come on, Collier. You knew my husband. It would be quicker for me to give you a list of his friends."

He looked up from his pad.

"You're wondering why I was attracted to him."

He didn't respond.

"That's a question I've been asking myself for more than a decade. I'm no closer to an answer now, than I was the night he proposed to me—the first time."

"But you *did* love him."

"I still do."

He believed her, and for a moment felt something akin to envy. No matter what his personal feelings were toward Underwood, the man had achieved something in his life that seemed out of Max's reach: he'd found unconditional love.

"Maybe I should rephrase my original question. Did you know of any of your husband's enemies who wanted him dead?"

She looked at Max with raised brows.

"Humor me," he said.

"Let me answer your question this way. My husband had his share of secrets. I can only guess what some of them were. Even now, I'm not sure that I really want to know. But I do know his death deserves justice. Are there any leads?"

He thought about revealing his belief that there might have been a witness, but he knew better. "No. Not at this time."

The judge picked up a kettle and filled it with water.

"Have you been to the DA's office? Maybe his death had something to do with a case he was working on."

"Checking that is definitely on our list," he assured her. He noticed that she had stopped making eye contact, and wondered what she was hiding . . . until he noticed her eyes had the glassy sheen that showed they were filling with tears.

"You know his boss couldn't stand him."

"D.A. Judith Mason?"

Judge Hickman nodded. "She wasn't too keen about me either."

Max already knew the story, but asked anyway. "Why do you say that?"

"Come on, Detective. I'm sure your partner has filled you in on his ex-partner, Jaclyn Mason, and her relationship to my husband."

Max killed the innocent act. "They were married once." He watched as Hickman's body stiffened and her movements became jerky.

"He realized he'd made a mistake," she defended.

Compared to the three he'd made with her? Max wondered, shaking his head to clear his negative thoughts. "I'll make sure that we talk to Mrs. Mason as well."

Sandra sighed and let her shoulders slump. "I doubt if she had anything to do with this. It's not in her character." She finally met Max's gaze again. "Don't mind me, I'm just reaching for straws."

He wanted to say, It happens. And it was true. Loved ones were often left struggling to make sense out of senseless crimes.

When he left the kitchen, he didn't have any more information than when he'd gone in. He hoped that his partner had had better luck with the search. He followed Hickman's directions to the den, and found Dossman poring over a book of some kind.

"Any luck?" Max asked, stepping into the room.

Dossman looked up briefly, then returned his attention to what he was reading. "I found a calendar. It's filled with names and numbers. I can't say that I recognize any of them."

"Were you supposed to?"

"I was hoping for a break, yes."

"What was on his schedule for Friday night?"

Dossman held up the book and pointed to an empty block. "Nada."

"Seems like we're on a roll."

Zone Five Precinct
Tuesday, 12:45 P.M.

Max slammed the phone down and released a long stream of profanities. No one knew, saw, or heard anything. "Isn't that just great?" He muttered.

"I take it we've hit another dead end," Dossman said, slouching in his seat.

"Gee, how did you guess?"

He laced his fingers together. "Let's just call it a hunch." Maybe we're looking too hard. We didn't find anything in Underwood's house or his office. Even his car, that we found parked two blocks from the crime scene, didn't turn up anything we could use."

"Yeah. But I'm not buying that the victim decided to take a leisurely stroll through one of the highest crime areas in the city." He thought for a moment. "I agree with you. We must be looking too hard."

"Okay, then let's start over." Dossman shuffled through the papers stacked on his desk until he recovered his worn notepad. "We know that on Friday Marion Underwood left his office at seven thirty-five P.M. We also know from the autopsy that the time of death was around midnight."

Max nodded while he pulled out a copy of the coroner's report. As he reread it he pointed to one item. "Where did he eat dinner?"

"Another mystery."

"According to the autopsy, he *did* eat."

Dossman failed to hide his irritation. "Do you have any idea how many restaurants are in Atlanta?"

"I'm not concerned about how many restaurants are in Atlanta. I'm only interested in how many are between Underwood's office and the crime scene."

"There's no proof that he had dinner at a restaurant. He could have gone to a friend's house, or some lady's house. According to Hickman, he didn't eat at home."

Max's brows rose as he studied his partner.

"What? There are still a few women out there who'll cook a homemade meal for their man."

"Then why hasn't she come forward?"

Dossman held up three fingers and counted the possible reasons. "Doesn't want to get involved. Wants to avoid suspicion. May be an accomplice to the murder."

"Okay, okay. I see your point."

"But do you know what's been bothering me about this whole thing?" Dossman met his partner's gaze as he leaned forward. "His car."

"What about it?"

"A top of the line Mercedes, left on M.L.K. for over twenty-four hours, and nothing was disturbed? What are the chances of that happening?"

"I wondered about that, too," Max admitted. "It made me think about who controls that area of town."

"Controls?" Dossman frowned, then slowly his eyes widened with understanding. "The Skulls."

Georgia Diner
Monday, 1:15 P.M.

Kennedy's head swam as she watched another news report regarding the slaying of ADA Marion Underwood. This time the coverage had made headlines on CNN. She swallowed the lump lodged in her throat, rushed to her locker to find some aspirins. With any luck, the pills would not only clear her headache, but also eliminate her guilt. The right thing to do wasn't necessarily the easiest.

"Kennedy, put some pep in that step. Your station is full." Bennie's booming voice shattered the silence.

She jumped and dropped the bottle of aspirins. "I'm coming, I'm coming," she said, kneeling to gather the pills.

A few minutes later, she returned to her station and resumed taking orders from impatient customers. All the while, she made sure she kept her smile bright and cheery. But, inside, her stomach twisted into knots.

How do you keep something like this a secret? she wondered, as her thoughts returned to the possibility of making an anonymous call. *Too risky.*

One of Kennedy's female customers screeched at her companion. "I don't care, Reggie. I don't want to be the last one there when this story breaks. Do you know what this could do for my career?"

"What about our source that said Collier's looking for a possible witness?"

"An unreliable source," she reminded him.

Kennedy assessed the woman with a quick glance and immediately classified her as high maintenance. "Can I get you two anything else?" she asked with a plastic smile.

"Yeah. A miracle witness to the ADA murder," came the woman's cynical reply.

The water pitcher slipped from Kennedy's hand. Its contents splashed everywhere, including all over Ms. High Maintenance's obviously expensive suit.

"You idiot!" The woman jumped from her chair and frantically wiped at the water-stained material.

"Ohmigosh. I'm so sorry." Kennedy's face heated with embarrassment as she scrambled to clean up the mess.

"What in the hell were you thinking about, you nitwit?"

Kennedy stiffened.

"Aaliyah, don't . . ." the woman's companion warned.

"Didn't you see what she just did, Reggie? Look at me."

"I *said* I was sorry."

"A hell of a lot that does me."

The women's heated gazes clashed.

Bennie quickly appeared and started doing what he did best: brownnose. "Ma'am, I'm terribly sorry for . . ."

Tired of having to put up with people talking to her like a second-class citizen, Kennedy turned to storm off, but was unprepared for the towering wall of muscular man that stood between her and the door.

She hit the floor and the wind rushed out of her lungs. Stars danced before her eyes for several dazzling seconds, and then cleared to reveal a breathtaking stranger.

"Are you all right, ma'am?"

Entranced by the man's seductive brown eyes, she hardly noticed his hand stretched out to help her.

"Ma'am?"

Kennedy blinked to clear the haze in her head. The sense of connection between her and the stranger intensified when she slid her hand into his and allowed him to pull her to her feet. It seemed as if every cell in her body reacted to him, forcing her to wonder who this strong and debonair man was.

"Detective Collier." The reporter's syrupy-sweet voice seemed to float in the air behind Kennedy.

Both Kennedy and Collier frowned.

A cop? He's a cop? "Excuse me." Kennedy said, trying to move around him.

"You're not even going to tell me your name?"

The man smiled and her knees buckled.

"Why? Are you arresting me?" She clamped her jaws shut and wanted to kick herself.

He crossed his arms. "Not unless you give me a good reason to."

His tone was serious, but his eyes were mischievous. Kennedy struggled to appear impervious to his charms. "I really have to go."

"Then it's my loss."

She answered his comment with a nonchalant smile. "I'm afraid so."

This time instead of storming away, she was convinced that she was floating away from the dashing detective.

Max's gaze remained focused in the direction that the beautiful waitress had gone. In the back of his mind, he questioned his attraction and couldn't come up with a logical explanation for it.

"So, Detective Collier, what brings you here?" Aaliyah asked, cradling her hands against her hips.

Max turned and couldn't force himself to smile. "I would imagine the same thing that brought you here: lunch."

With amazing grace, the reporter shrugged off his sarcasm and got straight to the point. "How is the Underwood investigation going?"

"Slowly." He paid the cashier for his carry out order.

"Any leads?" Aaliyah persisted.

He wanted to laugh at the woman's audacity. "Do you honestly think I would share any information with you?"

"Surely, we can let bygones be bygones?"

This time he did laugh. "You know, I'm not really known for saintly qualities like forgiveness. You burned me once. You won't get a second chance."

Once inside the break room, Kennedy decided that she'd had enough for the day. She was leaving.

A second later, Tyne, one of her co-workers, flew in behind her. "Girl, what's got into you today?" Her sentence ended with an annoying pop of her bubble gum.

"I'm fine."

"You sure don't seem fine to me. Hell, you have to be insane to turn that fine brother down."

Kennedy rolled her eyes heavenward as she snatched her bag from her locker. "Look, I just have a lot on my mind, okay?"

"I'll say." Tyne crossed her arms and drummed her fiery-red fingernails as she stood blocking the doorway.

Kennedy jerked on her jacket and tried to ignore her nosy friend.

"You know, you'd feel better if you talked about it."

I wouldn't even tell the pope about this one. "There's nothing to tell." She met Tyne's bold stare with one of her own. "I'm just tired."

Their gazes remained locked for an awkward moment before Tyne relented and tossed up her hands in surrender.

"All right. Suit yourself. I guess we all have our little secrets." She laughed. "Frankly, I've never liked that uppity reporter anyway."

"Reporter?"

Tyne's expression turned incredulous. "Girl, where have you been, under a rock or something? Everyone knows Aaliyah Hunter from Channel Eight."

Glancing at the door, Kennedy suddenly remembered the reporter's reference to the ADA's murder. In retrospect, she wondered how she'd forgotten it.

"Hello?" Tyne stepped into her line of vision and frowned. "Maybe you do need to go home and get some rest. You're acting strange."

Bennie poked his head around the door. "Any time you two feel like working, just let me know."

Tyne sighed. "Here I come."

Kennedy shook her head. "I'm out of here, Bennie."

He stared at his watch for a moment, then moved further into the room. At a robust six foot three, Bennie often made Kennedy think of a club bouncer. "You still have another hour left on your shift." His broad face reddened.

"I know, but I have to go. I'm sorry." She moved around him.

"What kind of business do you think I'm running here? Who's supposed to cover your station?"

"Look, Bennie. I've never done this before, I just need to get away for a while and think."

"Well, I'm doing some thinking myself. Like whether your services are needed here anymore."

Teeth clenched, she called his bluff. "You do what you have to do." She stepped around him.

He mumbled under his breath, but spoke up as she touched the door handle. "I expect you to come in here tomorrow with a better attitude."

With her back still turned to him, she smiled. "Deal."

It was dark when Max returned to the crime scene. Again he questioned what person in their right mind would perceive these eerie, desolate woods as a romantic hideaway. But carrying a high beam flashlight, he hoped to see or find something that they'd overlooked—something that might only be revealed in conditions similar to the time of the murder.

He reviewed his notes and considered several possible scenarios. The case was definitely a puzzle. He didn't mind that, since he loved challenges, but this one was missing a few pieces.

A quick glance at his watch confirmed that it was getting late and his frustration increased. At the rate things were progressing, the case could easily remain unsolved.

Max turned on his heel and had started to make his way back to his car when the beam of his flashlight illuminated an object nearly buried in the fallen leaves.

He walked over and knelt to extract a long silver chain. The first word that came to mind was dainty.

Maybe it belonged to some brave teenage girl who had ventured out here with her Romeo.

Max's curiosity heightened as he examined the uniquely designed locket that dangled from the chain. He turned it over to read the inscription:

> To my loving daughter
> and best friend.
>   P.K.S.

As he admired the piece, he suddenly wondered if he'd stumbled onto the first break in the ADA murder case.

Six

Kennedy tore through her bedroom, overturning clothes baskets, crates—anything she could get her hands on. All to no avail. "Where the heck is it?" She grumbled angrily. She stopped to touch her neck, halfway hoping that her locket would reappear.

It didn't.

Discouraged, she plopped down onto the edge of the bed and racked her memory, but she drew a blank. Her frustration rushed out in a long sigh. Nothing had gone right since . . .

She froze at the thought ". . . since the night of the murder." She propped her forehead against the palms of her hands and tried to concentrate, but details of that night danced just outside the realm of memory. Then, suddenly, she remembered twirling the locket on the bus while listening to Leroy as he recounted Mrs. Russell's woes.

Panic seared through her as her thoughts returned to that time in the woods. "Dear God, no." She stood, squeezed her eyes closed, and searched every crevice of her mind to remember whether she'd had the necklace any time since that dreadful night. Again, nothing.

The doorbell rang and Kennedy nearly jumped out

of her skin. Who would be visiting this time of morning?

The bell rang again and its sound was followed by an insistent, but melodious knock. She calmed immediately at the sound of that familiar rap, and even managed to smile.

She wasn't disappointed when she opened the door and saw her best friend. "Hey, Wanda," she said.

"Hey, girl." Wanda limped into the apartment without waiting for an invitation, which was the norm.

Kennedy frowned at the heavy cast on her friend's foot as she closed the door. "What happened to you?"

"That damn dog, Levi, is what. I tripped over him while cleaning the house. I don't know why I agreed to let Reece have one." Wanda eased onto one of the dining room chairs, ignoring the way it creaked beneath her hefty weight. "I swear that mutt doesn't do anything but piss all over my carpet and chew up what little furniture I own."

Kennedy laughed as she dashed into the kitchen to start a fresh pot of coffee. "Why don't you just take him back to the pound?"

A cigarette magically appeared in Wanda's hands, soon followed by the customary billow of smoke. "I'd love to, but every time I even think about it, he looks up at me with those big, sad, brown eyes and I find myself forgiving him for another smelly stain or rip on the sofa."

"I don't believe it. You're puppy whipped."

"What? That's not a real diagnosis." Wanda's face twisted with disdain as she reached to flick ashes into the only ashtray in the house.

"Sure it is. Levi has you wrapped around his paw and you know it," Kennedy teased, grateful for the opportunity to laugh and forget her troubles.

"You know there's an upside to me being in this cast." A slow smile crept across Wanda's lips, and her eyes got a mischievous glint.

Kennedy smelled a rat and proceeded with caution. "Like what?"

"Like I met this wonderful doctor. You're going to just love him."

Kennedy quickly held her hand out in front of her friend's face like a wall. "Forget it."

"Hear me out."

"No."

Wanda extinguished her cigarette, but not her prepared speech. "Come on, come on. This man is *perfect* for you. Now, I don't want to alarm you, but he *is* a little older."

"How much older?" She couldn't help but ask.

"Age is nothing but a number."

"How large *is* this unimportant number?" Kennedy shook her head when she realized what she was saying. "Forget that I asked. It doesn't matter, my answer is still no." She stood and returned to the kitchen to finish making the coffee.

"Girl, what are you waiting for?" Wanda called after her. "Prince Charming isn't going to just pop up and ring the front doorbell. And Lord knows that you never go anywhere to meet any eligible bachelors, so I'm giving you a hookup."

Briefly, Kennedy remembered the sinfully attractive detective she'd met at work. She smiled, and then quickly erased the expression. "My Prince Charming is currently in Pre-K."

Her friend shook her head. "You're going to turn Tommy into a mama's boy."

Kennedy's mouth fell open in shock. "That's not

true." Yet, her guilt increased with the accusation. She returned to the table and offered her friend a cup.

"Oh, yes, it is, and you know it." Wanda's expression turned sympathetic. "Look, don't get me wrong. At times, it's sweet how you dote on him, but how fair is it for you to hang all your hopes and expectations on a four-year-old? Face it, you need a man."

"Why do all married women think that single women need men to make them happy?"

"Because they do."

"They do not."

Wanda lit another cigarette. "Don't forget that I do have some experience with singlehood. I wasn't born married, you know."

"You could have fooled me." Anyone who knew Wanda and Walter Overton knew that they often behaved as if they were joined at the hip. It was sickening how they would finish each other's sentences or laugh uncontrollably at each other's stale jokes.

"Whatever, girl." Wanda reached into her breast pocket and produced a black and white business card and waved it in front of Kennedy. "It won't hurt you to go on one measly date."

For a moment, Kennedy actually reconsidered her position on the matter. She took the business card and studied it. "Dr. Anson Ward." She twisted her lips into a half frown. "He sounds kind of stiff."

Wanda's smile widened. "What else would a girl want in a man?"

Dossman relaxed as he watched his boss, Lieutenant Kelly Scardino, read and then reread his report. She drummed her fingers and the expression in her pale blue eyes reflected her disappointment. He smiled despite himself.

She looked up and pushed back a few graying blond locks before meeting his gaze. "Where's your partner?"

"He'll be right in. He was handling a few calls from the press when you called us in here."

Scardino flipped the report closed and tossed it onto a nearby stack of paper. "I'm not sure I want us taking any more calls from the media regarding the Underwood murder case. The press is already starting to make this investigation look like a circus."

Dossman bit back a cynical response and substituted a more politically correct one. "We're doing the best we can with what we have."

"It's not enough." She fixed her cool gaze on him. "Look, I'm getting a lot of pressure on this one. Then again, I don't know what the powers that be expect from us. We don't pull rabbits out of hats and we sure as hell don't perform miracles."

"Amen."

Their gazes locked and this time she smiled.

A quick rap on the door drew their attention a split second before Max entered. "Sorry about that, boss."

"It's okay," she said, pushing her chair back. "Have a seat, Collier." She stood.

He took a seat next to his partner. "What's up?"

"Well, for starters, I just finished reading Dossman's colorful report and I wanted to discuss where this investigation is heading."

"Into the toilet, if you ask me," Dossman said, crossing his legs at the ankle and staring up at his boss.

Scardino dismissed his sarcasm with a wave and directed her attention to Max. "What about you?"

"I think it's gang related, which, in itself, will make this a difficult case. Gang members don't usually roll over on each other. But, for the life of me, I can't imagine what kind of relationship existed between Underwood and a group like The Skulls."

"You think it's The Skulls?"

"They are the dominant group in that area," Max replied.

Scardino thought for a moment. "Have you shared any of this information with the Georgia Bureau of Investigation?"

"Not yet."

"Maybe there isn't a relationship between them."

"Come on, Lieutenant," Dossman argued. "There had to be something."

Scardino met Dossman's level gaze. "Maybe they were hired guns."

Maxwell observed the scathing looks being exchanged between his partner and Scardino and wondered at the source of their hostility. A lover's quarrel, perhaps?

The thought stuck him as odd. He smiled and dismissed the notion. Surely Scardino and Dossman weren't foolish enough to indulge in a forbidden and unethical affair. He shifted his gaze between them. Or would they?

"Okay." Max spoke a little louder than he'd intended, but his booming voice succeeded in slicing through the tension in the room. "I can see your point, Lieutenant. Someone hired The Skulls to do their dirty work. Sounds reasonable."

His brow shifted as he thought the scenario through. "It's going to be hard to find out who ordered the hit when we're not certain which members of the gang, if any, are responsible."

"Maybe we just need to follow our instincts on this one." Scardino crossed her arms. "Lord knows the facts aren't leading us anywhere."

"Whoa. This is a large gang. There has to be hundreds of those punks running around the city. Not to mention the ones living in surrounding states," Dossman reminded them.

"Then start at the top," she suggested. "Who's their head honcho here in Atlanta?"

Both men's eyes darkened as they responded. "Keenan Lawrence."

Scardino nodded in approval. "Find him."

Dossman gave a mock salute before jumping up from his chair. "We'll get right on it," he said and left the office.

Max started to follow his partner to the door, but stopped in the doorway, feeling a need to apologize for Dossman's strange behavior.

Before he spoke, Scardino said, "Don't worry about it. I'm used to Mike's antics." It was as if she'd read his mind.

The familiar manner in which she'd used Dossman's nickname heightened Max's curiosity about the pair, but he said nothing. He just smiled apologetically and shook his head.

When he returned to his desk, he retrieved the small plastic Ziploc bag containing the locket he'd found.

"I thought you were going to admit that into evidence?" Dossman said, plopping into the chair behind his own desk.

"It wasn't exactly discovered in the crime scene investigation."

"But I thought you had a hunch that it's connected?"

"I did . . . I do." He threw his hands up. "I don't know what I believe, actually. I think I'm still searching too hard on this one." He tossed the bag back down onto his desk.

Dossman lifted his brows as he studied his partner. Then, leaning his weight forward, he reached for the bag. "Pretty," he said, extracting the necklace. "It could belong to one of the promiscuous teenagers we've heard hang out in those woods."

"I thought of that, too."

Dossman opened the locket. "Well, I'll be damned."

"What?"

"What do you mean 'What'? Don't you know who this is?"

Max frowned. "Should I?"

"Come here." Dossman stood and gestured for his partner to follow.

Curious, Max did so.

When they reached the awards case, Dossman pointed to a plaque toward the back.

Max leaned closer, and then blinked in surprise as he noticed a duplicate of the picture encased in the locket he'd found. "Lieutenant Preston K. St. James," he read off the card beneath the photo. He smiled as he pulled his large frame erect. "I think it's time to pay a little visit to the lieutenant's daughter."

Seven

Kennedy sighed in relief when she arrived at her English class only to find that it had been canceled. Instead of being angry about having stayed up late working on her essay, she was grateful that she'd be able to crawl in bed early tonight.

As she waited at the bus stop, she couldn't stop worrying about her missing locket. If it were found, could it be traced to her? The blade of anxiety plunged deeper into her heart. She swore under her breath, tired of running over the list of fatal possibilities and constantly looking over her shoulder.

The bus arrived and Kennedy forced the negative thoughts out of her head. As she reevaluated the situation she had to laugh at herself. The chances that anyone could trace the necklace to her were slim.

Max slid into the passenger seat of Dossman's car and locked his seatbelt one-handed. Neither partner said anything until they'd pulled out onto the main road.

"Are you all right, man?" Dossman finally asked.

Max instantly relaxed his features, convinced that his troubled thoughts had chiseled lines into his face that had given him away. "Nothing I can't handle."

"That much I know." He shrugged. "I just thought that maybe you wanted to talk about it. I mean, we *are* partners—right?"

Max thought about denying that anything was wrong, but one downside of being partners with someone is that they tend to really get to know you. "Jacinda."

"Oh," Dossman nodded as if he finally understood. "I'd forgotten about your court date. I take it that things didn't go well?"

"No," Max's words were barely audible. He prided himself on controlling his emotions. That was something his mother had drummed into his head. "Men don't cry. Never show your emotions. Whatever happens in the family stays in the family."

When he'd been younger, the lessons had been hard to learn. But, as an adult, the controlled mask he often wore protected him from his stressful job and ugly divorce.

His ex-wife had often screamed that she hated that trait in him—hated how he could just shut himself off. He was cold and unfeeling, she'd sobbed. Had that been the reason she'd betrayed her marriage vows and then kept him from seeing his son, Franklin?

Max stopped that train of thoughts before it got any more painful and returned to the subject at hand.

"Actually, the whole thing seemed like a waste of time," he went on to say. "The judge acted as if she was on automatic pilot. She could care less that I'm a good father, or that I was the one who remained faithful." He looked out the side window, sweeping his gaze over the landscape. "I didn't do anything wrong, yet I'm the one being punished."

"It'll pan out. You'll see."

"I don't know about that." Despite the traffic, Max felt his partner's gaze on him. "Jacinda is getting married."

The statement hung in the air like a death sentence. Dossman finally emitted a low whistle. "When it rains, it pours."

"Tell me about it." With great effort Max suppressed the anger boiling through him. On top of everything else, he now had to face the real possibility of another man raising his son. "Life sure knows how to kick a man when he's down."

The silence that followed grew until Max broke it.

"I thought our routine went, I tell you my problems and you inflict bad advice on me."

Dossman laughed bitterly. "Trust me, I was all set to go through our usual routine, but you really floored me on this one."

Max shifted around in his seat to face his partner. "You know, as long as we're sharing things, is there anything I should know about you and Scardino?"

As he'd expected, Dossman's smile faltered, but the man's recovery was smooth.

"Not likely. I just like to rile her from time to time. She never takes me seriously though. Why you ask?"

"Just curious." Max made sure that he'd made his disbelief clear before turning back toward the window.

"This is it," Dossman informed him as the car rolled to a stop. He peered up at the building in front of them. "Not much to look at, huh?"

"Not really. But look over there." He pointed down the road. "The woods that concealed the crime scene."

"It's practically in her backyard."

Max nodded. "Let's go have a talk with her."

From the moment they stepped out of the car, it was clear that they stuck out like a sore thumb. Max felt, rather than saw, everyone's gazes on them.

"You'd think that we had the word 'police' painted across our foreheads," Dossman said, straightening his jacket.

"Yeah, you'd think."

They entered the brick building. Despite the age of the building, the walls were freshly painted and the carpet looked new. A few minutes later, they knocked on the door to apartment 8B and waited.

When they heard footsteps approaching, they remained on guard and prepared for anything.

"Who is it?" a feminine voice asked through the door.

"Police," Max answered in his best professional voice. As expected an awkward pause hung in the air, and both officers knew the woman was taking a good look at them through the peephole.

They heard the unmistakable thud of the deadbolt disengaging before the door opened a crack. The chain lock remained engaged.

"May I see some identification?"

Dossman and Collier took out their badges and held them up.

The door closed again and the chain was removed. When it opened again, they could see a petite girl who couldn't be more than seventeen.

"Is this the St. Jameses' residence?" Max asked.

The girl looked nervous, but she managed to nod.

Max lowered his gaze to the little boy hiding behind the teenager's legs. Despite the boy's youth, Max saw intelligence in his eyes.

"May we come in?"

The teenager stepped back and allowed them to enter.

"Are you Ms. Kennedy St. James?" Dossman asked.

"No, sir. I'm just the babysitter. Is there something wrong? Did something happen?" She closed the door behind them.

"Why are you looking for my mommy?" The little boy asked, lifting his chin fearlessly.

Max smiled. As he knelt in order to come down to eye level with the boy, he was startled by a strong sense of déjà vu. Those eyes were familiar. "We just wanted to talk to your mother—ask her a few questions—that's all."

The boy's gaze became more intense and Max had the funny feeling that the boy was trying to discern whether he was telling the truth. *Smart boy,* he thought.

"What's a good time to catch Ms. St. James?" Dossman asked the babysitter.

"She normally doesn't get in until late."

"About what time?"

"A little after midnight."

Both men nodded in satisfaction at that revelation. Max stood. "Is that every night?"

The teenager shrugged. "Pretty much, except on the weekends."

"What about last Friday? Were you babysitting for her last Friday?"

She hesitated before nodding.

"Did she get in around the same time then?"

"No. Uh, she came home kind of late—later than normal."

"How late?" Dossman and Collier asked in unison.

"About one o'clock."

Max and Dossman exchanged looks as Dossman mouthed the word "Jackpot."

Just then, a key rattled in the lock and everyone turned toward the door.

"Guess who's home," an unmistakably feminine voice sang as the door opened.

Max blinked in surprise as the familiar, angelic face of the waitress he'd met at the diner peered around the door. The woman stopped dead as she noticed him and his partner. Judging by her expression, she was none too pleased to see them.

Eight

Kennedy practically suffered a mini-coronary as she gazed at the two large men standing in the middle of her living room. She recognized one of them instantly from the restaurant. A cop. They were probably both cops. She stiffened, unsure what to do.

"Ms. St. James?" the handsome detective she'd met before asked.

She swallowed hard, and then answered in a thin whisper. "Yes." She knew he had recognized her by the way his gaze danced over her as it had at the restaurant.

As she lowered her gaze she caught sight of a brief smile that fluttered across his lips. Suddenly, she was incensed. "Is there something I can help you with, officers?"

"Yes, ma'am," the shorter man said, stepping forward, his confusion obvious from his expression as his attention shifted between her and his partner. "I'm Detective Dossman. I take it that you already know my partner, Detective Collier?"

"We've bumped into each other." Her tone flatlined. "Eve, go ahead and put Tommy to bed." She smiled down at her son and added, "I'll come in and read you a bedtime story in a few minutes."

Both Eve and Tommy nodded, then disappeared down the hall.

Kennedy returned her attention to the policemen. "Now, can I get you two something to drink?" She slid her bookbag from her shoulders and turned to hang it up on the coat-rack by the door.

"We just wanted to ask you a few questions, ma'am," Detective Collier reinforced.

Slowly, she turned to face him. "I can't imagine what for."

"It's about the murder of ADA Marion Underwood." He gave her the full measure of his solemn gaze. "I'm sure you've heard about it."

"I watch the news." *Cool. Play it cool.*

"Then you know that the murder happened not too far from here, around the time you usually arrive home."

"What a coincidence."

Collier's expression darkened. "I don't believe in coincidences."

"Pity."

Dossman crossed his arms as if he enjoyed the strained exchange between the couple. "Ms. St. James, what kind of car do you drive?"

Caught off guard, she flinched. "I don't have a car."

"Public transportation?"

She thought about lying. Maybe she should say that she usually caught rides with friends. But she knew that it was fruitless to lie about something so trivial and something that could easily be checked.

"MARTA is smarter." She quoted the city bus line's popular slogan.

Collier smiled, and took advantage of the opening. "Isn't the closest bus stop somewhere up on M.L.K.?"

Again she was forced to tell the truth. "Yeah, so?"

"So, you usually walk the rest of the way home?"

Kennedy drew in an angry breath, but managed to answer in a patient tone. "Yes."

"Mind if we ask which route you generally take?"

"I follow the main road where there are streetlights. A girl can never be too careful."

"You've never been tempted to just cut through the back woods?" Collier asked. "I'd imagine that it would be quicker—wouldn't you?"

"It might be. I wouldn't know."

"No?" He smiled and reached inside his jacket.

Heat rushed through her as she struggled to stifle the urge to slap his smug expression off his face. *Why did these men have to come here?*

"You wouldn't happen to know then, how this ended up in the woods?" He dangled the delicate locket in front of her.

Her breath hitched and she immediately realized her mistake. They'd caught her. Just like that. There was no sense in denying that the necklace belonged to her. No doubt it had been her father's picture that had led them to her doorstep.

"Ms. St. James?" Collier's smile had disappeared. Kennedy pulled her gaze from the locket and lifted it to meet his.

"You want to know what I think? I think that you didn't follow the main road last Friday night. I think you made a detour through the woods and saw something you wish you hadn't. Am I right?"

If she said yes, her world—her life would change. They'd want to drag her down to view a lineup. They'd make sweet promises they couldn't keep, or they'd die trying . . . just as her father had.

Max read volumes in the woman's delicate features.

Behind her cool, almond-shaped eyes, she was planning, thinking, calculating.

Amusement twisted the corners of his mouth. She was actually contemplating lying to him. He expected better from a cop's daughter.

"I don't know how that ended up in the woods." She reached for it, but he jerked it out of reach.

"I lost it months ago."

Anger made her even more beautiful. She lifted her chin as if daring him to call her a liar.

He smiled. "I'm relieved." Two could play her game. "Because, the way we figure it, there may be a witness to what happened to Underwood. Isn't that right, Dossman?"

His partner moved toward them and answered Max. "Uh, that's right."

"We also think"—Max's steady gaze returned to hers—"that whoever killed Underwood is quite aware of the existence of this witness."

"Yeah," Dossman jumped in. "Judging by the number of shots fired down there that night."

Kennedy swallowed.

"But we're glad to know that it wasn't you." Max gave his sarcasm free rein. "I'd hate to think that your life was in danger for being at the wrong place at the wrong time."

She narrowed her eyes. "You can stop playing games. I know what you're up to."

"And what's that?" Max challenged, crossing his arms to stare down at her. She had beautiful eyes, he realized. They were a unique shade of brown—light, with gold specks glistening in them. She glared at him.

Instead of answering, she turned and opened the front door. "I want you to leave."

Max's lips widened and Dossman actually laughed as they headed toward the door. "Are you sure you're making the right decision about this?"

Kennedy continued to glare at him, her expression motionless.

Dossman's hand dropped heavily against Max's back. "Come on, partner. Maybe we were wrong about this. Have a nice day, ma'am." With a confident smile, he sauntered out through the open door.

Max knew he was right. Not only did he feel it in his gut, but also he saw it in her eyes. He suddenly regretted how he'd handled this situation and tried once again to win her over.

"You know you can trust us. The police," he added when he saw her eyes widen.

"I think you were just leaving," she answered in a flat voice.

He reached inside his coat pocket and drew out a card. "Call me when you've had a chance to think things through. I'll be ready to listen."

The card remained perched between his fingers for an eternal minute, until she realized he wouldn't leave until she took it.

She snatched it, and he saw her jaws clench even tighter when he had the audacity to smile again.

"Have a nice evening, ma'am." His shoulders pulled back, drawing his frame into an intimidating height.

For a nervous moment, she shifted her weight on her Jell-O filled legs, but miraculously kept her chin up. "What about my necklace?"

The bastard had the nerve to widen his smile as he asked, "What about it?"

She held out her hand. "May I have it back?"

He laughed and she actually entertained the idea of bashing a vase or a frying pan against his thick skull.

He lowered the chain into her open palm, then closed her hand around it.

She sucked in an involuntary breath, astonished by the jolt of electricity that surged through her at his touch. Belatedly, she jerked her hand back, but it still burned—or tingled. That realization disturbed her.

"Goodnight," she managed to say, but her voice came out lower and wispier than she intended.

His smile vanished and his handsome face might as well have been made of stone. For a moment she had to resist the urge to caress his perfect profile.

"Call me." With that, he turned and vanished behind the door.

Kennedy closed the door, and then slumped back against it, her breaths slow and labored. What in the hell had she just done—lie to the police? Had she lost her mind? Her answer was an unequivocal *yes*.

The last twenty minutes replayed in the theater of her mind but, this time, her mind's camera focused more on the intensity of Det. Collier's eyes and the undeniable strength radiating from his towering frame. A war between her mind and heart ensued. Trust was what it all boiled down to . . . and she simply couldn't trust the police.

"Whoever killed Underwood is quite aware of the existence of this witness." Det. Collier's voice echoed in her head.

She felt the ice of fear trickle through her veins and her brain churned with great difficulty through her muddled thoughts.

If the police had been able to locate her, then how far fetched was it to suspect that The Skulls could, too?

From the way her heart pounded at the thought she suspected that, at this rate, she'd die of a massive coronary instead from a bullet from Keenan Lawrence.

Lord, she'd just run into the man on the bus the other day. Had that really been a coincidence? She was surprised to feel tears streaking down her face.

"Ms. St. James?" Eve questioned in a small voice.

Kennedy opened her eyes, as if she'd been caught doing something forbidden, and she hastily wiped her face dry. "Yes?"

Eve smiled as sympathy pooled in her eyes. "Tommy is waiting for you to tuck him in."

"Oh, yes. Thank you." She moved away from the door, her smile too heavy to lift.

"Are you all right?" the teenager asked.

The innocent concern on the girl's endearing face was Kennedy's undoing. Her tears rushed from her eyes at such a velocity that her vision drowned in its depths.

Eve's lithe arms encircled her, surprising Kennedy with their strength. Gratitude seemed too weak a word to describe what she was feeling—appreciation even worse. But, whatever word best suited the situation, Kennedy felt it tenfold.

Dossman hissed at Max, "Do you want to tell me what the hell you were doing up there?"

"What?" Max's feigned look of innocence clashed with Dossman's cynical stare.

"If she did see something, you just ruined any chance of her coming to us with her information."

"Oh, she definitely knows something. I'm more convinced than ever that she was there that night. I'm willing to bet my life on it."

Nine

After Eve went home, Kennedy tucked her inquisitive and, thankfully, sleepy son into bed with one of his favorite bedtime stories. Long after he'd fallen asleep, she remained perched on the edge of the bed, gazing down at him.

He was all she had left in the world—all that was truly hers. Now, through no fault of her own, she could lose that fragile gift. The ache in her heart was so profound she thought she'd die from it. Better that than to risk her child's life.

Kennedy leaned down and kissed Tommy's brow. He smiled in his sleep and she escaped from the room before another flood of tears broke free.

Alone in her kitchen, she wished that she was more than a social drinker. Alcohol would have been a great prescription for what ailed her. Then again it was good to have her wits about her while she tried to sort things out—come up with a plan.

Jerking open the freezer, she was disappointed that she hadn't replenished her banana strawberry shortcake ice cream and to hell with the low-fat version.

Grudgingly, she settled for one of Tommy's chocolate pudding pops as a consolation prize.

In a daze she entered the living room, her gaze

danced over the various items that made it home. But now something was missing—something unseen, yet tangible—security.

They weren't safe here anymore. That realization hurt.

"What am I going to do now?" she questioned in a soft whisper. Packing and getting the heck out of Dodge topped the list. In fact, they could leave tonight—now. But where would they go?

She returned to the kitchen for a second, third, then fourth pudding pop. They weren't half bad after all.

Somewhere between two and three A.M. she all but made up her mind to send Tommy to her grandmother's in Tennessee. Of course, Nana had only seen Tommy a few times. But that didn't stop the annual birthday and holiday cards.

Kennedy exhaled a long and tired sigh. A few minutes later, she yawned. Eventually, she surrendered her fight with the Sandman and drifted somewhere between the dream world and reality. . . .

She was back in the woods running, but this time there were no bullets flying. There were people. But instead of them chasing her, she chased them. Her parents ran just ahead of her; their musical laughter filled the air like a symphony.

They seemed so happy, so carefree, that she was envious. When they glanced over their shoulders to smile at her, their faces morphed into Lee's and Tommy's.

She started to run faster, and then suddenly her legs grew heavy—too heavy.

"Come on, Mommy." Tommy waved encouragingly.

She cried out, yet no words passed her lips.

Farther and farther, father and son ran. She feared that she would never catch up—feared that they wouldn't come back for her. Then, she would be alone. She struggled more vigorously. Her arms flailed in desperation.

"She ran this way," a hauntingly familiar voice instructed.

She turned to see Keenan wave on a group of men. Cloaked in black, eyes menacing, the men more closely resembled a pack of snarling Doberman Pinschers than a human gang. Her gaze fell onto the crossbones stitched on the men's front lapels and she realized that she would have preferred to face the dogs.

Kennedy stumbled, then struggled to climb back to her feet. Her limbs were so heavy . . .

"Mommy?"

A cool touch landed on her fevered brow and Kennedy's eyes flew open. Before she was able to discern the figure standing before her, she inched up the sofa with a startled gasp.

"Mommy, you're scaring me." Tommy's voice hitched—a sign that he was close to tears.

Kennedy's mind cleared and she pulled her son against her chest. "I'm so sorry, sweetheart. I didn't mean to scare you." She lowered her head to touch his.

"Were you having a bad dream?" he asked. His body trembled in her arms.

Her face felt damp. She lifted a shaky hand and felt the slick tracks of tears. It must have been a really bad dream. "It's okay. I'm fine now." She frowned when the dream drifted just beyond the realm of recall.

"Are you sure? You were crying and calling my

name." He rubbed his tired eyes with the back of his hand. His mouth stretched wide in a yawn.

"Come on. Let's get you back in bed."

"Maybe I should sleep with you so you can feel safe."

She laughed at the familiar quote. She used to tell him that whenever he had had a bad dream. "I don't think that will be necessary."

"Are you sure?" He could barely keep his eyes open.

She smiled at his weary but unquestionable chivalry. "I'm sure."

Max jerked open the fridge and withdrew a beer. He popped the cap and placed the cold bottle against his forehead. He closed his eyes and prayed for sleep. But as usual—his prayers had fallen on deaf ears.

He took a swig from the long-necked bottle and enjoyed the slight buzz he achieved from his fifth drink. Scratching the new stubble on his chin, he left the kitchen and returned to his La-Z-Boy.

Instead of reviewing his notes from the Underwood case, he reached for the silver frame that sat on the edge of the end table. He stared benignly at the small family smiling back at him.

Truth was, right now he didn't remember having that picture taken. He wasn't sure whether that was because of a bad memory or the effect of alcohol on an empty stomach. How old was little Frankie then— two, three?

"My, how time flies when you're having fun." He returned the photograph to the table. Problem was, he wasn't having much fun. He downed another long gulp, halfway wishing that this bottle would take him to oblivion—a place where pain didn't exist and nothing mattered.

He cursed under his breath. What was wrong with him? Oblivion was a temporary solution for a long-term problem. How on earth was he supposed to live with just seeing his son one weekend a month?

Max slid his gaze back to the picture, then narrowed his eyes at the woman who had ripped his heart out. Even sober he couldn't laugh at the memory of his once upon a time yearning for her— dreaming and planning on happily ever after. It was sickening really. Since then, willingness to trust or even love again had ranked in the bottom five hundred on his list of life's ambitions.

Another gulp and he emptied the bottle. He was no closer to oblivion now than he'd been five hours ago. Better luck tomorrow night.

In the fireplace, the once roaring fire had been reduced to glowing embers—such was his life. He waved off self-pity and depression with a sweep of his hand and grabbed the manila folder.

As his eyes peeled over notes and facts, he wondered *why* Underwood had been killed, instead of *who* had done it.

He shifted his gaze back to the fireplace. The embers brought back an unexpected memory of a certain pair of eyes that held their own kind of spark.

He smiled to himself, then worried about the truth of his own warning. How much trouble was Kennedy St. James really in? Did she understand what she was up against?

He remembered her little boy and thought more on his own son. It didn't take much to understand why she wasn't talking; to be honest with himself, he really couldn't blame her. But he had a job to do, and that job was to get her to talk.

Ten

Aaliyah rubbed her tired eyes and continued to stare at her computer screen. At this point, she wished that she could take her coffee intravenously to avoid the trouble of getting up to fill her cup.

She'd spent the last few days researching everything she could get her hands on regarding ADA Marion Underwood. Some articles painted him as a hero. Professionally, he'd won countless, impressive cases, ranging from domestic violence to organized crime. All were possible leads to his murder.

Then there were the articles regarding his personal life that portrayed him as a hypocrite, a liar, and a thief. Those were the ones that interested her.

Marion Underwood, born and raised in Atlanta, had been married four times: once to a cop, the other three to the same woman, Judge Sandra Hickman.

From what she could tell, his life hadn't become interesting until his second marriage. He'd wed a Det. Jaclyn Mason, a cop with all the right connections. The bride's father was Lieutenant Governor and her mother was District Attorney. How lucky could one ambitious man get? Though the marriage was brief, Underwood had emerged from it with a new job and a whole new lifestyle.

At dawn, Aaliyah decided to call it quits. Other than marital woes, she couldn't really find any dirt on the man, which was a great disappointment and meant that she'd wasted her time.

Another article appeared on the screen just as she was ready to log off.

FULTON COUNTY INMATE SCREAMS FOUL PLAY

Aaliyah leaned forward in her chair and read the date of the article. July 13, 1992. She reached for her mug and sipped absently at the lukewarm coffee.

According to the article, the inmate claimed that he'd been railroaded by the DA's office. He also pointed a finger at ADA Underwood for requesting a bribe.

The way the piece was written, it dispelled the inmate's ramblings as delusional and desperate. She quickly clicked another icon and pulled up all public information on the inmate, Keenan Lawrence.

Kennedy was dead on her feet. Dead asleep that is. By ten A.M. she'd declared the day a total disaster, which didn't leave much to look forward to.

She'd lost count of how many customers had deserted her station, fuming.

"Do I need to send you home before the lunch crowd swamps this place?" Bennie asked in a low and irritated voice. "You're not much help to me if you're going to be chasing away the customers."

"Cut me some slack. I'm in the middle of having a bad life. Do you mind?"

"By all means, go ahead. Don't let my measly little

business get in your way." His meaty hand covered his heart, but his look of sincerity was a mockery.

"You're a real piece of work, Bennie." She snatched the coffee pot from the burner and went to refill the cup of one of the diner's regular's, Mr. Riley.

"A penny for your thoughts," he said when he looked up at her somber expression.

"Why pay for what you can get for free?"

He smiled. "You got me on that one."

Kennedy returned the gesture, though the corners of her lips trembled a bit beneath the strain. "You're sweet for asking. Thanks." She patted his hand. "It's just one of those days."

Bennie suddenly appeared at her side. "Kennedy, when you two are done flirting, you might want to attend to the customers at table twenty-three. They've been waiting for ten minutes."

She clenched her teeth, wishing like hell she could bite him.

Bennie laughed and snapped a towel at her behind. "Get a move on it."

If she hadn't known Bennie for most of her life, and considered him a good friend, she would have reamed him a new one for that smack.

She arrived at table twenty-three and reached for her order pad without looking up. "Hi. Welcome to—"

Her mouth fell open when she raised her eyes and recognized her customers as Detective Collier and his smug partner.

"What the hell are you two doing here?"

Dossman frowned. "I'm willing to bet that you've never made employee of the month. Am I right?"

Her back stiffened. "Isn't this police harassment?"

Collier was a picture of innocence wrongly accused

when he looked to his partner and said, "I thought that this was called breakfast."

"Times are a-changing, I suppose," Dossman said with a shrug.

Kennedy controlled herself in time to stop herself from screaming a stream of obscenities. "Maybe this is a matter I need to take up with your superior." If nothing else, at least the threat sounded good.

"Does that mean that you won't be taking our orders?" Collier's innocent expression remained unchanged.

"You know, I'm starting to think your names should be Detective Abbott and Detective Costello."

"She has jokes," Dossman marveled.

"I've noticed."

Collier turned a smile in Kennedy's direction and she had to fight to suppress the butterflies in her stomach.

"You look like hell," Max said. "Didn't you get much sleep last night?"

The butterflies vanished. "I slept fine. Sorry to disappoint you."

"Hmm. I'm glad one of us did. I worried about you and your son all night."

She clenched her jaw and stared at him. "My son and I are fine." She flipped her order pad closed. "If you came here to pester me about that murder, then you're just wasting your time."

"Because you weren't there, right?" Max questioned.

She slapped her palm against her forehead. "By George, I think he's got it." Her expression hardened. "Now, if you two are finished wasting my time—"

"You haven't even taken our order," Dossman said, pretending to be insulted.

"Heck, we haven't even gotten a cup of coffee," Collier added. "Maybe *we* should have a word with *your* superior."

She stood there, infuriated, while they simply looked at her. "Fine. Two cups of coffee and then I want you two out of here."

Dossman glanced down at his menu. "And a ham and cheese omelet."

"Make that two," Collier added with a wink.

Delivering a left hook would no doubt land her in jail, but she entertained the thought all the same. "Two coffees, two omelets, anything else?"

"Toast," Dossman ordered as an afterthought.

"Bacon," Collier said, then snapped his fingers. "Better yet, make it link sausages." He shrugged. "You know what they say—breakfast is the most important meal of the day."

She couldn't manage a reply even if she wanted to. Instead, she turned on her heel and went to place their order.

Max watched her as she stormed off, unexpectedly drawn to the rhythmic sway of her hips.

Dossman waved his hand in front of Max's face to break the spell. "Earth to Collierville."

"Cut it out," Max admonished with an unexplained smile.

"Help me out with this one. I thought that you always played the good cop and I was the bad one," Dossman said.

"You're not sore, are you?"

"Of course not. I'm just wondering if this is the way we ought to go on this one. I mean, the object *is* to get her to trust us. Or, did I miss something?"

Max glanced around to ensure that Kennedy was out of earshot. "I don't think kneeling on bended knee is going to affect her."

"And playing like Columbo and pestering her to death will? I'm not following your logic."

Neither was Max, now that he sat back and thought about it.

When Max didn't respond, Dossman tried a different approach "Okay, let's do it this way. What's the plan? You *do* have a plan, don't you?"

"We have breakfast."

"That's it?"

"That's it," Max reaffirmed.

On cue, Kennedy returned to the table. The cups clinked as she sat them down.

"You wouldn't happen to have those cute little French Vanilla creamers, would you?" Max's smile dropped at her stony expression. "I guess Hazelnut is out of the question, too?"

Her hands balled into fists and nestled on her hips before she stormed off without uttering a word.

"I'm beginning to like her," Max said absently.

"Come again?"

His gaze swung back to meet his partner's. "Figuratively."

"Uh-huh." Dossman looked in the direction where Kennedy had disappeared, then back at his partner. "I don't think we're going to get her to talk this way. In fact, I think this is a lost cause. We have no real proof that she has ever been in those woods."

"What about the necklace?"

"She said she lost it."

"I don't buy it." Max waved a dismissive hand in Dossman's direction.

"I don't either. The point is that we can't prove otherwise."

"Then maybe we need to search harder." At Dossman's exasperated look, Max leaned over the table toward him. "I'm not just trying to be a hard-ass here. She's running scared. And what other option do we have? We can't turn our backs and make a wish upon a fallen star that we get another break in this case."

Dossman threw his hands up in surrender. "Okay, okay. You made your point . . . and I agree with you."

Moments later, Kennedy returned to their table. "Two ham and cheese omelets, toast, a side order of bacon, link sausages, and"—she reached into her apron pocket—"French Vanilla and Hazelnut creamers for your coffee. Please tell me there is *nothing* else I can get for you."

Both men smiled.

"Good," she said. She slapped their check down on the table, then headed for the next table.

"She does kind of grow on you," Dossman said with a wink.

After Kennedy made sure that all her customers were taken care of, she joined Tyne in wrapping silverware in linen napkins.

"I see your Romeo has returned." She nudged Kennedy with her elbow. "I should have known you were trying to pull a fast one on me. At least this time he brought a friend."

"Trust me. It's not what it looks like."

"Well, it looks to me like he can't keep his eyes off of you."

Kennedy followed her co-worker's gaze to the two detectives. She felt a strange fluttering again in the pit of her stomach. What was it about Det. Collier that affected her so?

The men noticed her and raised their coffee cups in salutation.

Annoyed, she ground her teeth and looked away. "I wish that they would leave."

"Mind if I take the shorter one?" Tyne asked.

"I thought you didn't go for the pretty boy type?"

"Girl, I go for just about any man with a job. I'll even settle for one who's at least looking for one."

Kennedy laughed. "You have issues."

Tyne shook her head. "I got bills, girlfriend."

Eleven

"Hey, Kennedy," Bennie called.

She looked up to see him waving her over. Before she took a step, she glanced over to table twenty-three.

Det. Collier and Dossman waved.

She moaned in disbelief.

When she approached Bennie, he looped an arm through hers. "Do your friends plan on being here all day? They're costing me money."

"They're not my friends."

"What—you recently started a fan club? They're sure as hell acting like they know you."

She sighed. "They're cops, Bennie. You're more than welcome to go and kick Atlanta's finest out if you want to."

His expression grew serious. "Is everything all right? Are you in some kind of trouble?"

Saying yes wouldn't change anything, nor would it help. It would only bring up more questions.

"It's nothing like that."

"Then what?"

"Nothing," she insisted and searched for a lie that would appease him. "They knew my father, that's all."

Bennie's expression displayed disbelief. He cast another glance at the two officers. "They look a little young to have been associated with your father."

"What are you, the FBI now?"

"Now calm down," he said, trying to placate her. "I was just saying—"

"Look, I'll just tell them to leave." She turned on her heel, ignoring Bennie when he called for her to come back.

As she drew near the table a funny thing happened. Her pulse quickened and her palms felt slick. When Det. Collier's head lifted and their gazes met, a sudden rush of heat surged through her. There was something about him that reminded her of her father. Perhaps it was the intensity of his stare, or the subtle character lines etched along his mouth and eyes. She wasn't sure.

To keep her wits about her, she decided to make and maintain eye contact with Dossman. In her opinion, he wasn't as intimidating as his partner. "Look, I'm going to have to ask you two to leave. My boss is giving me a lot of flak."

"Well, we can't have that." Dossman looked to his partner as if waiting for an objection.

"You know I'm really impressed with the service around here," Collier said. "Maybe we ought to have breakfast here every day, before heading into the office. What do you think, partner?"

Kennedy balled her hands at her sides.

Dossman shrugged. "It's as good a place as any, I suppose."

Kennedy turned then, sweeping her gaze over Collier like a searchlight. "Just what are you trying to do—get me fired? Is that how you go about coercing false confessions?"

Max showed obvious surprise at her outburst.

"Look," she said, slapping her hands down onto the table and leaning toward him. "I have a four-year-old I have to look after. I bust my ass waitressing two jobs and somehow still manage to scrape out time to go to night school. I don't have time to play silly games with you and your partner. I said it before and I'll say it again—I was *not* in those woods Friday night."

Disguised in a fake goatee and dark sunglasses, Keenan Lawrence smiled, and then took the last drag of his cigarette. He'd watched the fireworks exchange between Kennedy St. James and the two detectives with amusement. Though the small group had frequently talked in hushed tones, he'd always prided himself on his ability to read lips.

Whether the waitress was telling the truth, he didn't know. But he had every intention of finding out. The night he'd finished off Underwood, his men had come up empty when they'd chased the unexpected witness. But Keenan knew everything that went on on his streets, and he knew the regulars who traveled them. So he'd decided to do a little investigating on his own.

He'd seen Kennedy St. James from time to time, but knew more about her father than about her. And he should—considering that the man had arrested him more times than any other cop on the force.

"Can I get you anything else, sugar?" his waitress, Tyne, asked as she placed his bill face down on the table.

He lifted his gaze to the waitress and admired her pretty smile. "Nah, I think that will just about do me." He smiled back.

"Did you have just a little too much to drink last night?" she asked, dropping a hand to her hip, but continuing to smile.

"What makes you ask?"

"I don't know. You're wearing dark sunglasses indoors."

"I guess you got me." Keenan reached into his jacket. He watched the waitress's eyes widen when he withdrew a wad of money. The look in her eyes told him that she could be bought. "You know, now that I think about it, there *is* something that you can get me."

"You name it, sugar."

"Information."

District Attorney Judith Mason leafed through the remaining papers stacked on Underwood's desk. She half hoped that something would jump out at her— something that would tell her what had really been going on with her colleague. Everyone knew that there was no love lost between her and her ex son-in-law.

For years she had suspected that he was dirty—involved with God knows what. Yet, Underwood was a smart man. She'd remained convinced that he'd always stayed one step ahead of her and the authorities.

She tossed the papers back onto the desk and pushed back in the chair with a sigh of disappointment. There was a chance that she'd been wrong about him.

She considered the possibility carefully before she shrugged it off. Her instincts were too strong where Underwood was concerned. She was willing to bet anything that he was as corrupt as they came. But proving it was a different story.

She glanced at her watch. The police and the FBI would be arriving any moment. She gathered the folders she needed and headed to the conference room.

Detectives Collier and Dossman arrived promptly at one o'clock and Lt. Scardino, Captain Vincent, and two agents with the FBI shortly after.

"Now that we're all here, let's get started," she said with a brief smile. "As requested, I've gathered information regarding current case files Underwood had open, and prepared a list of the cases he'd finished or had been associated with in the past ten years. If you need access to anything on that list, you can call anyone here in the office and they will help you."

Max opened the manila folder he'd been handed and quickly scanned the contents. He shook his head. "May I ask you a few questions?" he asked, glancing up.

"Shoot." Judith crossed her arms and gave him her full attention.

"How was Underwood's behavior around the office in the days before his death?"

"Upon reflection, I would have to say he came across as if he was nervous about something."

"How so?"

"I don't know—he seemed distracted, jumpy even," Judith answered.

Scardino leaned back in her chair and asked, "Did you ever question him about it?"

"Actually, I did. Friday, the day of his murder, I made a point to stop by his office before I headed out myself. I remember, just before I knocked on his door, that I could hear he was in a heated argument with someone on the phone."

"Did you hear what he was saying?" Dossman said, joining in the questioning.

Judith shrugged her shoulders. "All I recall was hearing a stream of obscenities before he slammed the phone down. I knocked then, and entered when he barked for me to do so."

"And?" Max asked.

"He was clearly agitated and none too happy to see me at his door." She uncrossed her arms. "You see, Marion and I weren't exactly on the best of terms. I'm sure everyone in this office will tell you that."

"But you two have been able to work together for many years, haven't you?" Max leaned forward, keeping his gaze level with hers.

"Well, on paper, Marion Underwood was a good lawyer for the State."

"On paper?" he asked.

"How do I say this?" She looked away, struggling with her personal feelings toward Underwood. "It's nothing that I can point out physically. I can't hold up a piece of paper and say, 'See here, the man is dirty.' He was too smart for that. Yet, if you ever had anything to do with him—if you knew him personally—you'd know to walk away from him searching your back for knives. Does that make any sense?"

From the way people were nodding it made perfect sense to most of them.

"So, you don't think that we'll find anything in these cases?" Max asked, returning his gaze to the manila folder.

"In my opinion, no."

Scardino cut in. "Why is that?"

"Because I've already tried."

* * *

Max left the DA's office convinced that their investigation was stalled. He, like Judith Mason, didn't believe that they would find anything in the case information.

"So, what do you want to do now?" Dossman asked, sliding on a pair of Ray-Bans.

"Frankly, I think that our best bet is to stay close to Ms. St. James."

"I'm starting to think that you're developing quite a crush on the lady."

"It's not that." Max shook his head. "It's just a hunch that she's what's going to lead us to the killers."

Dossman's lips curved in a knowing smile. "It doesn't hurt that she's easy on the eyes, does it?"

Scardino stepped out of the building. Max looked up and smiled to himself. "I think you have your hands full with your own women problems. I figure the last thing you'd be concerned about is who I am or am not attracted to."

Dossman followed his gaze, and then swung back to look at Max curiously. "Now what's that supposed to mean?"

Max laughed heartily as he slid on his sunglasses and walked away.

Kennedy broke her routine and decided to take Tommy and Jimmy to Piedmont Park. She had all but made up her mind to send her son to stay with her grandmother, at least until things died down. As she watched him and his friend play Nerfball, she missed him already. It's only temporary, she assured herself.

She hoped that she was not overreacting—that

there was no real threat to her or her son—but she didn't want to take any chances.

"That's a nice kid you got there," the raspy voice said from behind her.

She jumped and pivoted on her heel.

Keenan Lawrence smiled, but his eyes did not.

Speech eluded her as her mind filled with images of doom.

"I take it you know who I am," he went on to say. He circled her.

"I've seen you in the neighborhood." She was surprised to have found her voice.

"Is that right?"

She nodded.

"That's good. I've seen you around, too."

She didn't respond, she couldn't.

"I knew your father, too. Did you know that?"

Kennedy shook her head, but it was a lie. Her father had hated Keenan—hated everything he represented. It had been no surprise to him when Keenan had risen through the ranks and become the leader of The Skulls. Standing this close to what she'd been raised to believe was the closest thing to the devil, she knew Keenan's being here wasn't a good sign.

"You must have this thing for cops."

"How so?" she chanced asking.

He shrugged. "I've just noticed them hanging around you a lot lately."

She cringed and cursed Det. Collier and Dossman for their carelessness. Their constant snooping might have just sealed her fate. "Why would you notice something like that?" She hoped she managed to look innocent.

"I make sure I know everything that goes on in these streets. That's part of my job."

An awkward silence grew between them as the gang leader continued to walk around her.

Kennedy stood still despite the fact her skin crawled. She clung to the hope that he wouldn't have the balls to kill her in a crowded park, in broad daylight.

"I can't see why you would want to watch me."

"Can't you?"

She shook her head. His words were like a sharp pin, puncturing her bubble of hope.

When he reached toward her, it took everything she had not to recoil. As he brushed back a wisp of her hair, the corners of his lips lifted again in a smile that looked sinister. "Did anybody ever tell you that you are a striking woman, Ms. St. James?"

She lifted her chin defiantly, struggling to comprehend the direction of their conversation.

"It's a shame for all this beauty to go to waste."

Puzzled, yet wary, she took a step back.

"How about a proposition?"

She didn't like the sound of that. From the corner of her eyes, she could see the boys were still playing, both oblivious to her dilemma.

"Are you going to ask me about my proposition?"

"I'm not interested."

He laughed, and the sound heightened her anxiety. "How can you say that? You haven't even heard what it is yet."

"I'm sure it can't be anything good."

He lifted his broad hands to cover what should have been his heart. "Now I'm hurt."

She said nothing.

He shrugged. "Look, I'm a businessman, plain and simple. And standing here, it just occurred to me that we can help each other out. I tell you what—it beats the hell out of waitressing."

Slowly she comprehended his offer. "Are you suggesting that I come work for you?"

Again he shrugged. "It's good money."

"You've lost your mind."

His smile vanished. "You think that you're too good to come work for me?"

Animosity radiated off him.

Kennedy took another step back.

"I think it would be poetic justice that the late, great, Supercop's daughter ended up on my payroll. Of course"—he stepped forward and returned his hand to her hair—"I have to test the goods myself."

In a panic, she turned away from him and raced toward the children. His malicious laughter rang in her ears. "Tommy. Jimmy. Get your things. We're leaving."

Twelve

"Mommy, are you all right?" Tommy asked, watching her as she threw his clothes into an old suitcase.

"Mommy's fine, sweetheart." Kennedy didn't break stride long enough to look up at her son. She had to hurry.

"Are we going somewhere?"

"You're going to go visit your grandmother. Wouldn't you like that?" She kept moving.

"Are you going, too?"

She stopped then. She realized that her son's voice sounded small and frightened. Slowly, she turned and sat on the unmade twin bed and waved him over to her lap.

He hesitated and looked as if he was on the verge of tears.

"Come here, sweetheart," she said, patting her lap. This time he came to her, his eyes wide and questioning.

Kennedy picked him up and placed him on her lap. "I wish I could go with you, honey, but I can't." Her tears threatened to surface.

"Why not?"

"For one thing, I can't afford it. I have to stay here and work."

Fat tears filled his eyes and rolled through his long curly lashes. "Did I do something wrong, Mommy?"

She hugged him to her. "No, baby. It's nothing like that."

He pulled back and looked at her as if he didn't believe her. "Then why do I have to go? Don't you want me here with you?"

Her vision blurred and tears trickled down her face. It felt as if her heart were being ripped from her chest. "If I had my way, I would never leave your side. But you're going to have to trust me on this, okay?"

He simply stared at her, his tears running down his small face.

"Do you trust me?" she asked.

He nodded without hesitation, but his obvious confusion remained. "How long will I be gone?"

"Not long, sweetie."

"How long is that?"

He wanted a definite answer to an unanswerable question. "I don't know, honey," she said, hugging him to her. "I don't know."

Over the next few minutes, Kennedy realized she had another problem on her hands. How was she going to get Tommy safely out of town without alerting Keenan or his street thugs? She didn't doubt for a minute that he knew everything that went on on his streets. And she had no doubt that he was making it a point to watch her.

Again she cursed Detectives Collier and Dossman. She was certain that their repeated appearances had attracted Keenan's unwanted attention to her.

The fact of the matter was that she was left with very few options, especially since she didn't own a car.

Jumping on MARTA with her son and a suitcase would be down-right stupid.

She thought of Wanda, but knew her husband would be at work and had their only car. She could ask Tyne, but she knew for a fact that if she did, little Ms. Busybody would show up asking too many questions.

She sent Tommy out to pick a few toys to bring along on his trip. While he rummaged in the living room, Kennedy paced the floor, distraught over her inability to come up with a plan. Then she thought of Reverend Warner. She trusted the reverend and his wife but, if her apartment was being watched, Keenan's spies would probably follow her son to the bus stop regardless of who took him.

Her stomach churned with anxiety. She didn't have the first clue about how to execute her plan.

Just then, Tommy came to tell her that the pot of water on the stove was boiling.

She managed to reward him with a wide smile and struggled not to weep. As she passed him in the doorway, she playfully pinched his cheek and went to finish fixing his favorite meal: hot dogs.

When she brought their food to the table, the sportscaster on the Channel Five news caught her attention. She found the remote and turned up the volume.

The day's baseball scores gave her the beginning of an idea. The Atlanta Braves had just beaten the Houston Astros with the score of eight to two. That meant the series was tied, two to two. The final game would be tomorrow evening at Turner Field.

Turner field, she thought, a person could easily get lost in such a large crowd. A slow smile curved her lips as she turned toward Tommy. "How would you like to see a baseball game tomorrow night?"

Scardino shook her head. "I don't know about this one, Collier," she said, sitting behind her desk. They had just briefed her about their suspicions involving Ms. St. James. "You have no proof that she saw anything."

"I have a hunch," Collier answered with a shrug of his shoulders. "Let me and Dossman tail her for twenty-four hours and see what we turn up."

"Then what?"

"If we come up empty-handed, then we'll try something else."

She drew in a deep breath, obviously considering his proposal. "If she was an accidental witness, I don't see what good tailing her is going to do. By your own admission, you don't think that she's a co-conspirator, so I don't see the point of surveillance. What do you think, Mike?"

Again with the Mike. Max turned amused eyes to his partner.

Dossman shifted uncomfortably. "I'm pretty much just along for the ride. Max says he has a hunch, and I don't see how it could hurt to just see where it leads."

"The way I see it"—Max brought the lieutenant's attention back to him—"I don't think that we're the only ones watching her."

She frowned. "You think The Skulls are watching her?"

"Dossman and I have both crossed paths with Keenan Lawrence before. He strikes me as a very smart man. I'm thinking that, if he's aware that there's a witness, he's going to pull out all stops to find out who it is."

"And you're sure that it's Ms. St. James?"

Max nodded.

Scardino bridged her hands beneath her chin, and then spread them out on her desktop. "All right. You have twenty-four hours." Her direct gaze centered on Max. "I just hope you're right about this. I don't like the idea of wasting time on this case."

He smiled. "Thanks. I'm sure you won't be disappointed."

"Let's hope that you're right."

Keenan took a seat across from his boss. Despite the confident air he'd hoped to convey, he looked nervous. He obviously didn't like the way his boss's two mesomorphic bodyguards stood behind him.

"Comfortable?" His boss's hard, clipped voice jerked Keenan's attention back to awareness of who was more important.

"Uh, yeah." Keenan adjusted his jacket while wondering why the lights were so dim.

"How about a drink—in celebration of a job well done."

He hesitated for a moment, knowing that poisoning was a real possibility. Yet, to decline could be equally fatal. "Sure," he said reluctantly.

"Good, good."

Almost instantly, two drinks were set on the table.

Keenan stared at the amber liquid for several heartbeats before his boss raised his glass.

"Cheers."

"Cheers," Keenan echoed, then tossed his head back, allowing the liquid to slide down his throat.

When he returned the glass to the table, his employer was staring at him with steel-gray eyes.

"Tell me, did everything go according to plan?"

Keenan shifted in his chair. He suspected that his boss already knew the answer to that question. "Pretty much." He refrained from elaborating.

The silence in the room seemed deafening. To Keenan, his heartbeat sounded more like a jackhammer, while his breathing was more like the rush of a tornado.

"Now, why don't I believe that?"

"You wanted Marion Underwood dead. He's dead. You left the details up to me."

His boss smiled. "True. But there has always been an understanding between us. No witnesses. How many men did you take with you?"

"Since when has the loyalty of my men ever been an issue?"

"Since *you* decided to execute a prominent lawyer, instead of making his death look like an accident. Yes, I left the details up to you, but I expected you to use your head."

Keenan glanced away, but said, "I had an old score to settle."

"Tell me about this potential witness I keep hearing about."

"I have that under control," he assured him.

"Do you now?"

Unaccustomed to having his word questioned, Keenan struggled to hold his temper. "You hired me to do a job, and I did it."

"A bit messy—"

"Leave the clean up to me. By this time tomorrow, that 'potential' witness will have drawn her last breath."

Thirteen

Turner Field
Friday, 6:45 P.M.

Kennedy stared, stupefied, at the teenaged girl in the ticket booth. "Fifty-six dollars? That's outrageous."

The teenager returned her stare, then shrugged. "We accept all major credit cards, or debit cards."

Kennedy looked down at her son and saw worry lines crease his face. He was too young for such an adult expression. She dug through her handbag.

As she searched for her elusive money, she heard a few people behind her grumble about her holding up the line.

Five minutes later, with tickets in hand, Kennedy and Tommy made their way into the stadium. Excitement lit the eyes of every child she passed as well as a few grown fanatics.

"Mommy, can I get a Braves hat?"

She looked down at Tommy and saw that the crowd's excitement had proven to be contagious. His eyes were wide and filled with wonder. It was his first visit to a professional ball game and Kennedy had never seen him so happy.

"Of course, sweetheart." As she smiled at his enthusiastic response, she had to blink away tears that flowed with the realization that in a couple of hours they would be separated—for a while.

By the time they'd found their seats, Kennedy had gone through another forty dollars. Between the tickets and the souvenirs and the food, she was nearly wiped out. Fortunately, she didn't have to worry about paying for Tommy's trip to Tennessee.

Mayor Bill Campbell threw the first pitch of the evening and, in no time, the game was under way.

While Tommy lost himself in the thrill of the game, Kennedy strained her neck to search through the crowd for a glimpse of Reverend Warner. She soon concluded that there was no way she'd be able to find the man in this crowd.

She took a deep breath and tried to mend her shattered nerves. The plan was to take Tommy to the men's restroom on the next level during the seventh inning stretch. The Reverend would be waiting there with a different set of clothes for Tommy. She didn't like to keep the kind man in the dark about what was going on, but she was thankful that he'd agreed to take Tommy to his grandmother without asking a lot of questions.

This is going to work, she affirmed, but still took another worried look around the stadium. Was Keenan out there somewhere, watching her? An unsettled feeling in her gut told her he was.

As Keenan put down his binoculars he couldn't shake the feeling that Ms. St. James was up to something. He, too, scanned the crowd wondering what or who she was looking for. Then he looked back at her. Maybe she was wondering if he was there.

He smiled confidently at that thought, but still he wondered.

Max lowered his binoculars and shook his head. "She's up to something." He took another look and noted Kennedy fidgeting and taking frequent glances at the crowd.

"What do you think it is?" Dossman asked, taking a bite of his hot dog.

"I wish I knew." Max glanced around the exuberant crowd and shook his head again. "I wish I knew."

Reverend Warner was nervous. He didn't understand the need for this cloak and dagger plan of Kennedy's, but she'd made it clear that she believed her son's life was in danger. That was enough to motivate them into action. Besides, they were driving up to St. Louis for their daughter's wedding anyway, so it would be simple enough to drop Tommy off at his grandmother's.

"Do you see her?" Linda Warner asked her husband, clutching his arm.

"Not yet."

She fumbled with the bag containing the spare clothes they'd borrowed for Tommy from the church's charity donations. "I have a bad feeling about this." She looked around. "Do you think anyone's watching us?"

The reverend gazed lovingly down at his wife. "Why would anyone be watching us?"

She shrugged. "I don't know." She exhaled. "Like

I said, I just have a bad feeling about this whole thing."

"Would you have preferred that I'd told Kennedy no?"

Her eyes lowered. "Of course not."

Rev. Warner draped a supportive arm around his wife, and placed a kiss against her worried brow. "Hang in there. It won't be long before the seventh inning."

At the bottom of the sixth, the Braves were at bat. The score was tied three-to-three. The first two batters struck out on their first three pitches. The third batter had started off in the same pattern, and the call was standing at 0 and 2 when the first two balls were called strikes.

The crowd hushed as the battle between the pitcher and the batter intensified. The next two pitches appeared to be in the strike zone, even from the cheap seats, but they were hit foul.

Kennedy wiped at her sweat-slick hands. One more out and it would be time to execute her plan. Several small beacons of doubt surfaced in her mind as she wondered if she had covered every possible scenario that could go wrong. She nibbled at her bottom lip as she realized everything that could go wrong would. What if Reverend Warner wasn't here? Maybe he'd been called away on business and couldn't make the game. It was possible. After all, he was a busy man.

The batter swung and connected as the pitch crossed the plate. It was a base hit up the middle.

Tommy jumped up and down and waved wildly, joining in with the crowd's cheering.

She smiled as she watched him point excitedly to

a giant styrofoam hand with the raised index finger that proclaimed number one. She wished that she had thought to bring him to a ball game before now.

The crowd went wild when the next batter made a base hit on the first pitch.

Kennedy glanced at her watch and took another look around. Her anxiety grew.

The next batter hacked at his first pitch. Then, on the second one, the fans jumped to their feet as what had looked to be a potential home run drifted foul. The crowd moaned in disappointment.

Tommy slurped his drink, but never took his eyes off the game. When this was all over, Kennedy vowed she'd sign him up for T-ball for next spring. Who knew, she just might have had a little athlete on her hands.

She smiled at the thought, and was surprised that she could manage it under the circumstances.

On the next pitch the suspense ended. The batter struck out, leaving two men stranded. The inning was over.

"Are you ready?" she asked Tommy with a nervous smile.

High in the stands, an organ played the introduction to "Take Me Out to the Ball Game."

Tommy nodded and rose to his feet. "Will I still get to see the end of the game with Reverend Warner?"

Kennedy placed a silencing finger against her lips, but nodded.

He smiled, but she read his sadness at leaving her clearly in his eyes. She wanted to pull him into her arms and assure him again that their separation would only be temporary. Instead, struggling to keep everything looking normal, she took him by the hand, stepped out into the aisle, and led her young son toward the bathrooms.

Keenan bridged his hands beneath his chin as he watched the mother and son move through the crowd. Gone were his earlier apprehensions that his quarry was up to something. She was more likely just nervous about being out in the open.

C-note, one of Keenan's most trusted gang members, leaned over in his chair and asked, "What do you want us to do, boss?"

Weighing his options, Keenan knew that, in a case like this, being surrounded by a crowd was more of a blessing than a curse for a gunman. People tend not to take much notice of their surroundings and the shooter had the luxury of blending in with the crowd. If he was going to make a move, now was the time.

Keenan nodded as he made his decision. "Kill them both."

Fourteen

"Is that who I think it is?" Dossman said, peering through the binoculars and then handing them over to Max.

"Where?" Max asked.

"Over there." Dossman pointed him in the right direction.

"I don't recognize anyone. Who am I looking for?"

Dossman grabbed the binoculars back. "Let me see those." He looked again but the man he'd spotted was gone. "I could have sworn—"

"Who did you see?" Max asked as he turned his gaze back to where Kennedy and Tommy had been sitting. They were gone.

"Lawrence," Dossman finally answered. "I could have sworn I saw Keenan Lawrence."

"What?" Max rose from his seat. The combination of Dossman's sighting and Kennedy's sudden disappearance frightened him. "Come on, we've got to go. Kennedy's gone."

"Go where? I thought you were watching her."

"Will you just come on?" Max pushed into the throng marching toward the concession stands. He *had* been watching. He'd only looked away from her for a moment.

Once they reached the concession area, Max's hopes for finding Kennedy dipped. There were hundreds of people milling about. It would be next to impossible to find one particular mother and child.

"Any ideas?" Dossman asked, craning his neck as he searched through the crowd.

"Let's split up. If you find either Kennedy or Keenan, stick to them like white on rice. Something is definitely about to go down."

Kennedy pushed through the crowd, stepping around everyone who got in her way and keeping Tommy's hand in an unbreakable grip. Just when she thought she'd never reach her destination, she caught sight of it just in front of her.

She glanced down and smiled encouragingly at her son. She wanted to go into a big spiel about how good he should be at his grandmother's, and how soon they'd be together again. The problem was that, if she did start such a speech, she would quickly burst into tears.

Tommy looked up at her then. In his gaze, she saw all the things she was feeling: love, uncertainty, and fear.

She knelt before him and pretended to tie his shoelaces. "I'll call you tomorrow at grandma's," she told him, then leaned forward and kissed his round cheek. "I love you."

"I love you too, Mommy," he said, returning a tentative smile.

Kennedy blinked several times and willed her tears not to fall. She stood and glanced back toward the men's room to see if she could see any sign of Reverend Warner.

"I can go in by myself," Tommy assured her.

"No, wait right here with me. I'm sure the reverend will be here at any moment."

He frowned, obviously hurt that he wasn't being given the opportunity to prove that he was a big boy.

Kennedy pinched his cheek, but right now even that kind gesture seemed to embarrass him.

"Mom," he whined. "Not in front of all these people."

She laughed. "All right. How about we get a soda while we wait?"

He nodded and smiled again. All the while they stood in line at the concession stand, Kennedy kept the door to the men's room in her view. Her mental list of "what ifs" began replaying and anxiety churned in her stomach.

"Well, what do you know?"

Kennedy pivoted at the unexpected sound of a familiar baritone voice.

"Fancy meeting you here," Det. Collier said with a wide smile.

Kennedy frowned. "Go away."

He laughed and rested a hand on her shoulder.

Her entire body tensed. It was then that she noticed that his laugh rang differently in her ears. Instead of meeting her eyes, she noticed that his gaze skittered through the crowd around them.

"What's wrong?" She turned and tried to figure out what he was seeking in the crowd.

"You're being followed," he whispered from behind her.

"You mean, by someone other than yourself?" She glanced again toward the bathrooms. With her suspicions confirmed, her worry escalated to full blown fear.

Danger hung in the air, thick and heavy. Something was about to happen—she could feel it.

Before she could do anything, her arm suddenly erupted with an unexpected surge of pain. Her eyes widened with shock.

"Get down!" Collier looped his strong arm around her waist.

They stumbled together toward the ground, as she heard something whiz past her injured ear.

A woman screamed.

The initial impact with the cement floor knocked the wind out of both Kennedy and Collier.

Then all hell broke loose.

The crowd's screams reached Dossman's ears. He pivoted on his heel, his weapon drawn. He rounded a corner where he'd last seen his partner and was momentarily blocked by a stampede of people.

"Police," he shouted as he tore through the crowd, but his shouts went unheard amid the rising cries of hysteria. Whatever progress he thought he'd made getting through the sea of people vanished when reality settled and he soon realized that he was being pushed backward with the flow of traffic.

A stream of curses rumbled from his chest. What he wouldn't give to be able to fire a warning shot. Perhaps that would bring some order to the madness. Instead, he had to struggle to move sideways, to inch along the wall. He returned his gun to his holster, and managed to reach the wall only after receiving his fair amount of elbowing and shoves.

Amid the chaos, he was shocked to catch a glimpse of a familiar face. "Keenan." Indecision spiraled up his spine briefly, then Dossman took off in the opposite direction, and thankfully, along with the herd of people.

"Are you, all right?" Max shouted. His entire body covered Kennedy's in an attempt to protect her from whoever was shooting, and also from being crushed by the rampaging crowd.

She squirmed and clawed as she tried to get up from beneath him.

"Hold still. I can't protect you if you keep trying to get up."

His reasoning fell on deaf ears, as her struggle grew more desperate. "Please, Kennedy, please. Just lie still."

Her fist landed sharply against his chin and he was momentarily surprised by her strength. But she would need a lot more than that if she wanted to actually do damage.

She screamed a name and he heard her anguish and desperation as it tore from her throat.

"Tommy."

Max's eyes darted around. Where was the little boy? Had Tommy been with her when he approached her in line? He searched his memory. He wasn't sure.

"Kennedy, where is he?"

"Don't let them get my son."

"Where is he?"

She didn't answer, she just continued to flail her arms about, occasionally landing punches. She was ignoring whatever injury she'd sustained from the bullet, despite the growing stain of blood on her sleeve.

He tried to gain control of her hands. When he succeeded, he shook her to get her attention. "Damn it, Kennedy. Pull yourself together and tell me where he is."

"The men's room," she finally said. "That's where he was supposed to meet the person who was helping us. I'm sure that's where he'd go when we were separated."

Max darted a quick glance at the restroom across from the concession stand, then looked around the area. The crowd was thinning, but there was no way to know if their shooter had made his escape yet, or was still waiting to finish the job. There was no way he was leaving Kennedy's side, so they'd need to work together to find Tommy and get to safety.

"Okay, Kennedy. I need you to do what I say."

She hesitated, obviously not trusting him to share her priorities. She shifted her gaze to the men's room.

"In just a moment, we're going to get up together and make our way to the men's room," he said.

She nodded, but it didn't stop him from worrying about the sheer terror radiating from her eyes.

"I'm going to try to shield you with my body as we get up."

She started to get up and he had to restrain her.

"We get up together, understand?" he shouted.

She flinched from the roar of his voice, and then nodded in agreement.

Max retrieved his weapon, kept his head ducked low, and simultaneously swept his gaze around the perimeter.

As they stood, they were pushed and shoved by the screaming crowd.

Kennedy blinked tears from her eyes. When Collier slid his arm securely around her waist, a certain calm fell over her. She felt protected.

Collier jerked her to his left side. She felt the rush

of something whiz by and saw it puncture the plastic casing at the concession stand.

Someone was still shooting at them.

Kennedy trembled. It wasn't that she was afraid of dying; she feared that she'd be responsible for Tommy's death as well. Had the gunman gotten to him? What about Reverend Warner—was he dead as well?

It took what seemed like an eternity for Collier and Kennedy to reach the bathrooms, but at least there were no more shots. As they reached the door, she bolted from his grasp and entered the men's room, leaving him to stand guard against whoever was shooting at them.

Empty.

Frantic, she searched the stalls. "Tommy? Tommy?"

Again, empty.

"Is he in here?"

Kennedy jumped at the sound of Collier's voice, but she didn't answer. She checked all of the stalls again, praying that she'd missed the one Tommy was hiding in. But he wasn't there.

Collier rushed into the room—a look of panic monopolized his face.

The room seemed to tilt and Kennedy could actually hear the sound of blood rushing through her head. Tommy was gone and Kennedy had no clue as to who had him: Rev. Warner or Keenan Lawrence.

Fifteen

Aaliyah Hunter pushed away from her desk in her home office after reading Keenan Lawrence's file. The man had danced into and out of jail his entire life. Fame came the moment he'd risen through the ranks of one of Atlanta's most notorious gangs: The Skulls.

Even after learning all of this, Aaliyah had found nothing that helped her with her investigation of the Underwood murder. Intuition told her that she was on the right track. She moved over to the computer and tried cross-referencing the two names.

Three cases came up that involved both Underwood and Lawrence. The first one she'd read about yesterday. The second one had occurred in '93, a murder case. Apparently, it was a drug deal that went bad. The arresting officers, Detectives Jaclyn Mason and Kenneth Nelson . . .

Aaliyah recognized the names and pulled out her notes. Jaclyn Mason had been Underwood's second wife. She flipped through more papers to find out the dates of their marriage. According to her information, the case was tried during their marriage. She frowned and wondered what it all meant . . . if it meant anything at all.

* * *

Max watched as Kennedy's face drained of color and she seemed to teeter uncertainly on her legs. He rushed to her and caught her just before her body hit the floor.

"Kennedy." He gave her a firm shake. He couldn't believe it, she'd passed out.

"Come on, sweetheart. Wake up." He propped her up, lowered her head between her knees, and spoke firmly and clearly. "Come on. You need to wake up."

She moaned and managed to sound irritated at the same time.

He looked around and noted that there were two entrances into the bathroom. They couldn't stay here much longer. The gunman could come charging in at any second. He shook her gently. "Kennedy, wake up. We're not out of danger yet."

"They got my baby," she said in a choked sob. The pain in her voice jerked his heartstrings. Though it was not an appropriate time for it, he wanted to console her and make the pain go away.

Something moved out of the corner of Max's eye and he dropped with Kennedy and rolled to his right side. The room exploded with the sound of bullets slamming into the concrete.

Kennedy's screams pierced Max's eardrum as her entire body quaked against him. With perfect speed, agility, and aim, Max returned fire.

The gunman crashed against the wall. His weapon fell from his hands as a look of surprise was etched into his features.

Max dropped his head back against the floor and stared unblinkingly up at the ceiling. It took several deep breaths to slow his heartbeat and clear the scenes from his short thirty-two-year life span that had passed before his eyes.

Only then was he able to remember the woman who still quivered in his arms. Her ragged sobs dissolved, but she clung to him as though her very life depended on it.

Lowering his weapon to his side, he pushed them up into a sitting position. He draped his arms around her. As she rocked back and forth, he whispered words of comfort, while wondering wildly what had happened to Thomas St. James.

Keenan strode confidently along with the crowd. By now, C-note had done his job and his troubles were over.

A heavy hand landed on his shoulder.

Keenan reached inside his jacket.

"Unh-unh-unh," a man warned from behind him.

At the unmistakable feel of a gun pressed against the center of his back, Keenan clenched his jaw. A cop.

The man's free hand fumbled with Keenan's jacket, before he found and removed the Glock that was the gang leader's favorite weapon.

"I hope you didn't think that you were going to get away with that little stunt you pulled back in there."

"I don't know what you're talking about, officer," Keenan said, his voice thick with sarcasm.

"I just bet you don't."

Keenan smiled, his old cockiness returned. "I hope you're not going to try to pin that shooting in there on me."

"Can't see why not. You went to great pains to sneak a weapon onto the premises."

"It hasn't been discharged."

There was a pause as the cop checked out his claim.

"A small technicality. How many cronies do you have inside working for you?"

Keenan laughed. "You cops are all the same. You all want to be Dirty Harry or something. Can't a man just come and enjoy a baseball game?"

The cop slapped on the first circlet on Keenan's left wrist, but, before his second wrist was secured, Keenan spun and kicked.

Dossman had no time to react when his own gun went flying into the air. He reached to retrieve Lawrence's gun from inside his jacket, but the movement took too long and Keenan had already drawn his backup weapon.

The first bullet entered Dossman's shoulder. Despite the intensity of the pain he was obviously feeling, the man still reached for the Glock.

Keenan fired again.

His target jerked into the air, then slammed against the pavement. He didn't move again.

Sixteen

Alone, Kennedy sat in a hard wooden chair in the interrogation room. She held a cup of hot coffee, halfway hoping that its warmth would penetrate her bones and stop her shivering.

She guessed that she'd been at the police station now for about an hour. Detective Collier hadn't asked her too many questions. He seemed more concerned about her welfare and state of mind than anything else. But she knew the hard-hitting questions would come. She just didn't know what she was going to tell him.

She sipped her coffee, but didn't notice its taste. In her mind she remembered the awkward smile she shared with Tommy moments before all hell had broken lose. Had he entered the bathroom on his own, or had he been snatched from right under her nose?

Kennedy closed her eyes. She wanted to believe more than anything that Reverend Warner had him and they both were long gone by the time hell broke loose inside the stadium.

But what if he wasn't?

Thoughts of the alternatives overwhelmed her. She set her cup down onto the table with more force than she intended, causing coffee to slosh over the rim and burn her hand.

"Damn." She waved her hand back and mentally cursed her stupidity. What would she say when Collier eventually asked about her son? Did she dare to trust the police?

Glancing at her watch, she wondered how much longer she would have to remain cooped up in the small room. She was already beginning to feel as though the walls were closing in on her.

What if Keenan had her son? By choosing to keep her mouth shut, she might be endangering Tommy's life.

With her head resting in the palms of her hands, she gripped chunks of her hair and actually considered pulling them out.

Just then, the door swung open with an intimidating whoosh. Kennedy stiffened and became instantly alert. Judging by the fierce, haggard look on Det. Collier's face, she predicted the pity party was over.

"Let's see if we can take this from the top," he said, pulling the chair opposite her out. When he sat, his eyes took on an intensity she hadn't witnessed before.

She forced herself to shrug. "I can't think of anything to tell you that you don't already know."

For a moment, she wondered whether he'd heard her. When he finally responded, his voice was low— edgy. "I don't know whether you can tell or not." His eyes met hers. "I'm not in the mood to play games with you."

Kennedy swallowed. She could definitely tell. She

started to speak again, thought better of it, and then closed her mouth.

He drew in a deep breath and leaned back. The wooden chair creaked under his weight. "Good. Now that we've eliminated the b.s., let's take it from the top. Why would someone go to so much trouble to try and kill you, Ms. St. James?"

Kennedy pressed her muted lips together. Her skin felt hot beneath his glare. Through the room's suffocating tension, she almost expected him to lunge across the chair and strangle her.

"You're trying my patience, Ms. St. James."

Again she remained silent.

Det. Collier slammed his hand against the wooden tabletop.

She jumped, but swallowed her scream of alarm.

"I have half a mind to haul you down to a jail cell—"

"On what charges?" She jerked her head up, the fire suddenly ignited by her own breaking point.

"I kind of like the sound of conspirator to the murder of ADA Underwood."

"What? You must be joking."

"Am I?" He leaned toward her. "My partner is fighting for his life at Grady Hospital because of you. I should lock you up for the next twenty-four hours just because I'm in a bad mood."

He could do it too, she realized. She swallowed again, but the lump in her throat enlarged. She searched his hard features for signs of compassion— heck she'd even settle for pity for her plight.

There were none.

Her shoulders slumped as the past week's stress and frustration escaped her body in a long sigh. "Then I guess you're going to have to arrest me."

Det. Collier jumped up. His chair screeched back like a locomotive. "Fine."

Some small part of her died when her bluff failed and she watched him stride angrily toward the door.

"Don't you understand that I'm dead if I talk?"

Max stopped, but he didn't immediately turn around. "You have it wrong. You're dead if you don't talk to me. Or did you misunderstand what tonight's shootout was all about?"

"My son . . ."

When she failed to complete her sentence, he turned and met her opaque, yet even gaze. She looked frail and defeated. He hated himself for adding to her misery, but there was nothing he could do about it. She'd backed him into a corner. How could he protect her when she insisted on tying his hands?

"I'm sorry about your partner," she whispered.

He found himself nodding and allowed a cloud of worry to drift across his troubled thoughts. "He's a good cop. A good man."

He continued to stare at her. As he waited for her to say more, his gaze danced over the subtle details of her face. Before, he had noticed the richness of her almond-shaped eyes. He couldn't think of a man who wouldn't drown in their depths—including him. Right now, however, he noticed the long lashes that framed her eyes as she stared down at her hands. Then there were her lips. If he had to describe them in one word, it would be fascinating.

In his humble opinion, she was simply the most beautiful woman he had ever met. And something in him died as he witnessed her shrink into herself.

"Let me ask you something, Ms. St. James." He intentionally lowered his voice and removed any trace of sarcasm. "If I were to release you right now, how long do you think it would take for Keenan Lawrence and his army to get to you?"

She jerked at the mention of Lawrence's name and Max gained a grain of satisfaction from knowing that his theory was correct.

A dark and troubled shadow fell over her. It was clear that she hadn't thought that far ahead and she grew smaller by the second.

"I can take care of myself," she answered in a whisper that sounded nothing like the spitfire he'd met two days ago.

"No, you can't."

Their gazes met again and he wished like hell that he could read her thoughts—wished that he knew the magic word that would get her to place her trust in him.

Kennedy was the first to pull her gaze away. "I have no choice." And she believed that, but she had no idea how she planned to survive this.

"What about your son?"

"He's safe," she answered with a nod of her head.

"You don't know that."

"No," she said. "But I have to believe it."

It was Max's turn to drop his head. Kennedy St. James was as stubborn as she was beautiful, an irritating discovery.

The room fell silent again as Max searched his mind for some type of compromise he could offer, but could find none. "I can't let you walk out of here, knowing that you won't make it to see the sunrise." He looked up.

Her gaze fell and she bit her lower lip in concentration. He wondered if she was thinking where she could lie low. Were there friends that could take her in and protect her? Judging by the way her eyes suddenly brimmed with tears, he concluded that she had no one she could depend on.

He was starting to think that locking her up for the night was the only way he could protect her.

What would happen to Tommy if something were to happen to her? Sure, her grandmother would try to raise him, but she was nearly eighty. She wouldn't be able to care for him for long.

She tried to think of another solution, but that was difficult to do under Collier's tight scrutiny.

"Kennedy?"

She lifted her head at the tenderness he used when he called her by her first name. This time, when their eyes met, she saw empathy in his expression.

"You have to trust me."

For first time since they'd met, she wanted to trust him; wanted to share her burden and receive some type of protection from this craziness she'd found herself in.

Collier retrieved the chair he'd abandoned and placed it in front of her.

Kennedy followed his every move. She caught the faint scent of his cologne and when he spoke, she heard the exhaustion.

"What can I do to get you to trust me?"

She didn't have the answer to that. She didn't have an answer to anything. "I just need time to sort all this out," she said truthfully.

"We don't have the luxury of time."

Her eyes brimmed with tears. She closed them, ashamed that she'd lost control of her emotions.

His hands encircled hers and an undeniable warmth spread throughout her, and had an amazing affect on calming her fears. She resisted the urge to lean forward and rest her head against the broad span of his chest, as she had done earlier at the stadium.

In that singular experience, she had cried until all her tears were spent, and a peace she had never experienced had settled in her soul.

"You can't go home," he said softly. "You realize that, don't you?"

Kennedy nodded.

His fingers gently rubbed the palms of her hands, and something tingled at the base of her spine then spiraled upward.

She pulled her hands away, troubled by what she was feeling—what she had felt since the day she'd laid eyes on him.

He frowned, and then sighed. "Okay. We'll play this your way. It's painfully obvious that I'm not going to get you to talk, am I?"

"I can't, not until I know that my son is safe."

"And when will that be?"

She remembered when the Warners were due to drop off Tommy. "Noon tomorrow."

Collier nodded. "All right then. Then we have to hide you for"—he looked at his watch—"twelve hours. I have a suggestion."

Hope flashed as she stared up at him.

He held up a hand, as if expecting her to reject his idea. "It's the only way I can keep an eye on you while you wait to find out about your son."

Suspicion replaced hope, and Kennedy waited for him to drop his bombshell.

Max met her direct gaze. "I think you should spend the night at my place."

Seventeen

A waterfall of tears cascaded down Lieutenant Kelly Scardino's face as she looked down at Dossman's motionless body. The doctors had assured her that the worst was over. The rest was up to Dossman and his will to live.

She stared at him, unnerved by his coloring. Their last argument echoed in her mind and a sour taste formed in her mouth. Marriage. He had actually proposed marriage.

The cocky laugh she had given him died in her throat. If she'd ever doubted that she loved this man, she stood corrected. She slid her hands toward his, and cringed at the lack of warmth they possessed.

What had she been thinking when she'd turned him down? The small voice in the back of her head answered clearly and succinctly. Her career. She had been thinking about her career.

Shame swept over her, along with regret. She wished that she could turn back the hands of time and change her answer.

She focused on their hands. Their colors were different and beautiful.

Dossman's eyes fluttered open and, for a moment, confusion reflected in their depths. Then he focused on the woman by his side and a lazy smile curved his lips. "Well, well, well. Look what the cat dragged in," he said, then licked his parched lips.

"You should look in a mirror," she teased and squeezed his hand.

He laughed, then winced as pain shot through his chest. "Damn, did I survive the hit or not?"

"What do you think?"

"It sure doesn't feel like it. It feels like someone drove a Mack truck through me."

"I'd say, judging by the size of the hole in your chest, that's a possibility."

"Were you worried?" His smile widened.

Her expression grew somber. "You know I was."

"Really?" he asked, surprised that she'd come clean so easily. "How much?"

Tears crested and followed the previously laid tracks.

"Hey." He lifted a trembling hand and caught one of her tears in mid-stream. "There's no need for these. I'm going to be just fine."

She nodded as her smile wobbled. "I know you are."

"Then what's with all the tears?"

"They're for us."

Dossman took a deep breath, and this time ignored the pain that caused. "Are you planning on dumping me again?"

She laughed. "I don't think so. After what happened tonight, I doubt that you'll be able to shake me any time soon."

"That's always good to hear."

She looked down, played with his fingers as she spoke. "I keep thinking about the other night."

"Kelly—"

"Let me finish," she said with a stern look. "I keep thinking about the other night, and thinking that I made a mistake."

"Don't do this to yourself, hon. These type of situations always seem to elevate—"

"Elevate what I already feel for you—have felt for a long time."

Dossman's gaze caressed her face—a face he had spent the last two years loving. The adoring look she gave him touched his heart and made what he had to say that much harder. "I don't think you made a mistake, sweetheart."

Fresh tears glistened in her eyes and he tightened his grip on her hand.

"Everything you said the other night made sense. If we let anyone know about us, it would cost you your career."

She shook her head.

Dossman continued. "You've worked too hard to throw all that away now."

"But I'm not willing to throw us away." She pulled his hand up and placed it against her heart. "That's what I'm trying to tell you. If I have to choose, then I choose you."

Dossman felt his own tears begin to surface. "You'll regret it. I don't ever want you to resent me, and that's exactly what you'll end up doing. Maybe not today or tomorrow. But you will."

Her tears fell in earnest and Dossman patted his right shoulder for her to lay her head. When she did, he held her and shed his own tears.

"You want me to do what?" Kennedy's eyes rounded with astonishment.

"Do you have a better idea?"

Her forehead furrowed as she searched for another solution. Her short list of friends ran through her head. Sure they would take her in, but not without asking a lot of questions. And if she involved another party, would she be placing their lives in danger, too?

Collier frowned. "Surely, you don't think I'd harm you?"

"It's not that." She clamped her mouth shut, unsure of what else she should say. She couldn't tell him that she was beginning to question her body's response to him, or that she enjoyed those feelings.

"Then what is it?"

"Look, I just don't think that it's a good idea." She shrugged, aware that she sounded juvenile.

Collier tossed up his hands. "I give up. I shouldn't have to convince you to save your own life. But, if you don't care, I don't see why I should."

Again, he bolted from his chair and headed toward the door. "You're free to go, Ms. St. James."

The door slammed shut behind him and Kennedy jerked in response. She closed her eyes during the ensuing silence.

"Free to go," she whispered. But she didn't move—couldn't move. She didn't know what waited for her outside that door. She opened her eyes, wondering how he'd managed to suck the oxygen out of the room when he left.

As minutes passed, she questioned why she still sat there, staring at the door. But, in her heart, she knew the answer. She wanted Collier to come back.

Slowly, she forced herself to stand and retrieve her purse. She had no idea where she was going, but there was no sense in staying there.

She put her hand on the doorknob, took a deep breath before pulling the door open.

Det. Collier waited with his hands crossed on the other side. "Are you ready to go to my place?" he asked.

She stared at him for a moment, and then nodded.

Keenan clenched his teeth as he paced the floor in long, angry strides. Tonight's screw-up would cost him plenty, and bring unwanted scrutiny from the men in blue. That, in turn, would bring heat from his boss.

He swore under his breath and resisted the urge to throw something—anything. Nothing had gone right in the past week. The last thing he needed to do was to shoot a cop—in front of hundreds of witnesses. He cursed his foolish actions.

"You're slipping, ole boy," he mumbled under his breath. As he waited to hear the word on the officer—a Detective Dossman, according to the news reports—he tried to plan his next move. He definitely needed to lie low, perhaps even skip town until everything died down.

He shook his head. He didn't like the thought of leaving town with unfinished business. Kennedy St. James.

He stopped pacing.

The woman either had an angel on her shoulder, or she was just lucky as hell. Twice she had slipped through his grasp. That wasn't an easy feat to pull off. He should have killed her at the park when he'd had the chance.

He paced again.

If he was going to take care of her, he needed to do it quick. Getting out of town would be easy, finding Ms. St. James would be a challenge. And one thing he loved was a challenge.

He smiled.

Eighteen

Det. Collier opened his apartment door and gestured for Kennedy to enter. "Ladies first," he said with a smile.

With an unexplained nervousness, she crossed the threshold and immediately heard the click of a lightswitch behind her.

Bright lights bathed his spacious living room that was decorated with black leather furniture and little else.

"Forgive the mess, the maid is on vacation," he joked as he closed the door behind them.

She glanced around again, and saw a few empty beer bottles on the coffee table, along with a stack of paper. Other than that, the place appeared immaculate. If he considered this a mess, she wondered what he thought of her apartment.

The awkward silence between them grew as they stood near the front door. Then Collier remembered his manners. "Ah, I guess I should show you my bedroom."

She jerked around to meet his gaze.

"I'll take the couch," he added.

She nodded, suddenly embarrassed by the direction

her thoughts had gone in response to such an innocent remark.

"Of course," she said. Then she followed him across the living room and down the hallway. Still glancing around, Kennedy thought it was odd that there weren't any pictures of any kind on the walls, or any knickknacks on the shelves.

"Just moved in?" she asked, absently.

"Yeah, about a year ago." He entered a room and switched on the lights.

She peeked in and saw only a king-sized bed. Again, there weren't any pictures; heck there wasn't even a headboard or a bedside table.

"Are you sure you live here?"

"Did the last time I checked." He smiled. "If you'll hold on for a moment I'll get you some clean sheets."

She nodded, then moved further into the room. While he was gone, she noticed an adjoining bathroom and a closed door to what she assumed was the closet. Overall, the room was less than homey—way less.

Collier returned, carrying a set of folded white sheets.

"I'm starting to feel like I'm staying in a hospital, Detective Collier."

He laughed. "Please, I'd say, given the circumstances, we should at least be on a first name basis. Call me Max."

"All right, then, *Max.* I feel like I'm staying in a hospital. White walls, white sheets . . . do you have anything with a splash of color?"

Again, he laughed. "You know, my mother taught me that beggars can't be choosers."

Kennedy's hands jumped to her hips. "I'm no beggar, Detective Collier."

"Max."

"I'm no beggar, *Max.*"

He shrugged, but his eyes twinkled. "I'll get you a set of sheets with color."

She couldn't help but smile.

After the sheets were changed, Max handed Kennedy a set of pajamas he had just bought a couple of days before. The flannel pajamas were still in the store's plastic packaging. Kennedy took it along with some clean towels—again white—and headed off to the shower.

Not until she stood beneath a steady stream of water did she realize how much her body ached and how much she wanted to cry.

After stepping out of the shower, Kennedy toweled herself dry and stared at her reflection in the mirror. The first thing she noticed was how old she looked. She leaned closer and touched the bags under her eyes and wondered when she'd developed them. She dropped her hand from her face, and shook her head. Life was doing a number on her.

Kennedy tore the plastic off the new pair of pajamas. She stepped into the pants then laughed at how they swallowed her body. Not only was there no chance the waistband would cling to her small hips, the legs were so long her feet were buried in enough material to make an additional pair for Tommy.

The top wasn't much better. While it fit her like a midlength dress, the shoulders were too wide and the sleeves too long.

After several attempts to tie and fold the material to make the pants fit, she gave up on them and decided to just wear the pajama top.

As she stepped from the bathroom and turned off the light, she heard a rap at the door.

"Yes?"

"Are you decent?"

She laughed. "It's as good as it gets, I suppose."

The bedroom door opened a crack and Max stuck his head through. When he caught sight of her, he laughed.

"Ha, Ha. Where do you shop anyway, the Jolly Green Giant's closet?"

He shrugged. "Beggars can't be—"

She cut him off with a hard glare.

"All right, all right. I just came to ask if you were hungry. I could eat a couple of horses myself."

"Where are we going to get something to eat at three in the morning?"

He pushed the door further open and made a dramatic bow. "Chef Maxwell Collier at your service."

She crossed her arms and asked with a measure of disbelief, "You cook?"

"Madam, I do more than that. I create masterpieces."

Her skepticism lasted a few seconds, before her stomach's loud growl answered for her.

"I guess I'll take that as a yes." He winked.

She turned her head, in the hope that he wouldn't notice her flustered look, and caught sight of a white phone sitting on the floor by the bed. She turned back toward him. "Can I join you in a few minutes? There are a few things I want to take care of."

"Sure."

Kennedy watched as his jovial expression faded, but was surprised when he didn't ask any questions.

"I'll see you in the kitchen in a few."

She nodded and waited until he closed the door before she rushed over to the phone. She punched in the Warners' phone number, and then nervously

twisted the phone cord while she waited for the line
to connect.

On the fifth ring, she reached the answering machine. She listened to Mrs. Warner tell her that they
weren't in and to please leave a message. At the beep,
she hung up.

She stared at the phone and somehow managed to
resist the urge to cry. *He's all right. He's all right.* Kennedy closed her eyes and clung to her affirmation—
her hope. At this moment and time, it was all she
had.

When she opened her eyes and took in her surroundings, she thought the vast emptiness reflected
how she felt inside. She'd lost so many important people in her life that she couldn't fathom losing her
baby. What would she do if she did?

Kennedy shook her head and refused to delve into
that possibility. Her stomach growled and she remembered Max in the kitchen. Hopefully, once she ate
something, she'd able to crawl into bed and snatch a
couple of hours of sleep. She stood and gazed at the
bed and knew that she was fooling herself. There was
no way that she was going to get any sleep tonight—
or any night. Not until she knew her son was safe.

"Soup's on," Max called from the kitchen.

Kennedy went to join him in the kitchen. "What
smells so good?" She froze at the kitchen door,
stunned at the sight of Max before her.

He was dressed only in a pair of black flannel pajama pants. He stood, stirring a pot on the stove. His
bare, muscular chest drew her gaze like a magnet and
invited her imagination to explore a world of possibilities.

He turned and faced her. It was his frown that
jolted her from her deep reverie.

An important message from the ARABESQUE Editor

Dear Arabesque Reader,

Because you've chosen to read one of our Arabesque romance novels, we'd like to say "thank you"! And, as a special way to thank you, we've selected four more of the books you love so well to send you for FREE!

Please enjoy them with our compliments, and thank you for continuing to enjoy Arabesque...the soul of romance.

Karen Thomas
Senior Editor,
Arabesque Romance Novels

Check out our website at
www.arabesquebooks.com

3 QUICK STEPS
TO RECEIVE YOUR "THANK YOU" GIFT
FROM THE EDITOR

Send this card back and you'll receive 4 FREE Arabesque novels! The introductory shipment of 4 Arabesque novels – a $23.96 value – is yours absolutely FREE!

There's no catch. You're under no obligation to buy anything. You'll receive your introductory shipment of 4 Arabesque novels absolutely FREE (plus $1.50 to offset the costs of shipping & handling). And you don't have to make any minimum number of purchases—not even one!

We hope that after receiving your books you'll want to remain an Arabesque subscriber. But the choice is yours to continue or cancel, anytime at all! So why not take us up on our invitation to receive 4 Arabesque Romance Novels, with no risk of any kind. You'll be glad you did!

Call us
TOLL-FREE
at 1-888-345-BOOK

THE EDITOR'S "THANK YOU" GIFT INCLUDES:

- 4 books absolutely FREE (plus $1.50 for shipping and handling)
- A FREE newsletter, *Arabesque Romance News*, filled with author interviews, book previews, special offers, and more!
- No risks or obligations. You're free to cancel whenever you wish... with no questions asked.

BOOK CERTIFICATE

Yes! Please send me 4 FREE Arabesque novels (plus $1.50 for shipping & handling). I understand I am under no obligation to purchase any books, as explained on the back of this card.

Name _____

Address _____ Apt. _____

City _____ State _____ Zip _____

Telephone ( ) _____

Signature _____

Offer limited to one per household and not valid to current subscribers. All orders subject to approval. Terms, offer, & price subject to change. Offer valid only in the U.S.

Thank you!

AN051A

Accepting the four introductory books for FREE (plus $1.50 to offset the cost of shipping & handling) places you under no obligation to buy anything. You may keep the books and return the shipping statement marked "cancelled". If you do not cancel, about a month later we will send 4 additional Arabesque novels, and you will be billed the preferred subscriber's price of just $4.00 per title. That's $16.00 for all 4 books for a savings of 33% off the cover price (Plus $1.50 for shipping and handling). You may cancel at any time, but if you choose to continue, every month we'll send you 4 more books, which you may either purchase at the preferred discount price. . . or return to us and cancel your subscription.

THE ARABESQUE ROMANCE CLUB: HERE'S HOW IT WORKS

PLACE
STAMP
HERE

ARABESQUE ROMANCE BOOK CLUB
P.O. Box 5214
Clifton NJ 07015-5214

"I'm sorry, what did you say?"

"I said, I hope you like soup."

"Soup?"

His frown transformed into a smile.

Kennedy crossed her arms and tapped a bare foot on the linoleum floor. "What happened to you creating masterpieces?"

His smile widened. "Now this isn't your ordinary, run of the mill soup. This is my grandmother's special recipe."

"Your grandmother's recipe?"

"Yes, ma'am. She's the best cook this side of the Mississippi."

She stared at him for a moment, then had to admit, "Well, it does smell pretty good."

"If you think that's something, wait until you taste it." He turned and reached into a nearby cabinet and withdrew two bowls.

As he prepared everything, Kennedy couldn't help but think that his giddiness reminded her of a child's. It was obvious that the man loved to cook.

He placed the steaming bowls of soup on the dining room table, and then went back into the kitchen to get spoons.

Kennedy sat down. "Do you have any salt and pepper?"

He stopped and looked as if she had kicked him. "You haven't even tasted it yet."

Suddenly, Kennedy felt as though she had grown two heads. "I always use—"

"Trust me, you won't need it." His smile returned as he joined her at the table.

She couldn't help but return the gesture. Closing her eyes, she leaned over her bowl and inhaled the heavenly aroma. "Mmmm."

"Good, huh?"

Her eyes fluttered open and their gazes met. A warm, sweet sensation coursed through her. She swore that she was drowning in the dark pools of his eyes, and swore that it took more effort to breathe in his presence.

He lowered his gaze and the spell broke. "Go ahead and give it a try," he said, not quite sounding like himself. He obviously noticed the difference, too, and cleared his throat.

Kennedy dipped her spoon and tasted Max's "masterpiece." She blinked once, and stared at her empty spoon.

"Well?" he probed.

She tasted it again, then eyed him suspiciously.

He continued to watch her expectantly.

Kennedy picked up her napkin and threw it at him. "This is Campbell's soup!"

Max kicked back in his chair and a hearty laugh rumbled from his chest.

"I don't believe you." She wished she had something else to throw.

His laugh deepened and tears seeped from the corner of his eyes. "I had you going there for a moment."

"You can't cook, can you?"

"I plead the fifth," he said, wiping his eyes.

"I just bet you do, Chef Collier."

"Aw, come on. You're not mad at me are you?"

"I knew that you were full of it. Canned soup is probably all you can handle."

"I resent that."

"But you don't deny it?" Kennedy rolled her eyes and gave him the silent treatment.

"Okay. I'm sorry. I thought that you could use a

good joke." He sobered as he added, "Especially after the day you had. I just wanted to put a smile on your face." He reached out and grasped her hand.

A familiar jolt of electricity surged through her. She met his gaze again, and then smiled. "Well, you succeeded. Thank you."

Max's gaze caressed her face. "The pleasure was all mine."

Nineteen

Max and Kennedy finished their dinner in silence, but not without their share of secret glances.

Kennedy couldn't remember the last time she'd shared a meal with someone of the opposite sex, four-year-olds excluded. She had reached a strange level of intimacy with Max—being in his home, wearing his clothes.

She stole another glance at him, took in his bare chest and smooth complexion. How long had it been since she had enjoyed the touch of a man? When was the last time she'd lost herself in the folds of a man's embrace?

Memories of Lee Carney surfaced and Kennedy smiled down at her soup.

"Now that's a smile," Max observed.

Kennedy blinked; then her face grew warm with embarrassment. The reaction only fueled his curiosity.

"Come on. What are you thinking about?"

"It was nothing."

"It sure didn't look like nothing. You looked like the cat that swallowed a coveted canary."

She shrugged, then flashed him a quick smile. "Women are allowed to have secrets."

"Secrets, eh?" He stood with his empty bowl and

reached for hers. "Are you through with that, or are you going to continue smiling at it all night?"

She handed him the bowl. "Here. I can't eat another bite."

"I hope not. That was your fourth serving."

"You counted?"

His brows rose. "You didn't?"

"All right, all right. So I was a little hungry." She laughed. "What's the matter? Are you running low on canned goods?"

"Hey, you should know how much a cop makes. It's enough to make a grown man weep. Trust me."

"So, why do you do it?" she asked with genuine interest.

"What do you mean?"

"I mean, if you're unhappy about the pay, then why are you a cop?"

He shrugged. "I guess because my old man was a cop and I thought he was the coolest guy on earth."

"Really?"

"Yeah. I mean, when I was young my pop would come home late at night and regale us with stories about the good guys versus the bad guys. It all played like a comic book adventure in my head."

"It's in your blood, huh?"

"Bad." He cocked his head. "Your father was a cop. You were never tempted to join the force?"

"Not just no, but oh hell no."

He laughed.

"You don't understand," she said. "My father may have been a highly decorated officer but, deep down, he hated his job. He hated what he saw on the streets night after night. He often told me that the job stole any hopes he had for the country and for our people. One part of our community is fighting for the right things and the right causes, while another part is busy destroying what we've achieved."

Max nodded. "He was right."

"He usually was."

Max took the dishes into the kitchen. "Can I get you something to drink?" he asked, opening the fridge.

"What are my choices?"

"Let's see. I have water, beer, water, did I mention beer?"

She shook her head and stood. When she leaned against the archway, she crossed her arms. "As soon as I get a chance, I'm going to pray for you."

"What?"

She laughed at his feigned look of innocence. "You know what? Since it's been a while since I've had a chance to behave like an adult, I think I'll take a beer."

"All right. Now we're talking."

The phone rang just as he handed her a bottle.

"Excuse me," he said and picked up the wall unit in the kitchen. "Yeah."

"I thought you were coming back to the hospital?" Lieutenant Scardino's voice came over the line.

"Sudden change of plans. I'll have to tell you about it later. How's he doing?" Out the corner of his eyes, Max watched Kennedy move away from the kitchen to give him his privacy.

"He's awake and doing good."

Max detected a note of sadness in her voice. "That's definitely good to hear." He hesitated, not knowing how much he could or should say. "How are you holding up?"

There was a long pause and he suddenly wished that he had ripped out his tongue.

"I'm not sure," she answered in a wavery voice. "In the back of my head, I always knew something like this was a possibility, but I never prepared myself for it."

"No one can. But hey, Dossman is a strong man. If he made it this far he's going to be fine, right?"

"That's what the doctors are saying."

The line fell silent again, but he sensed that she wanted to say more. When she finally spoke, her tattered emotions rattled her vocal cords. "I love him, Max."

His heart squeezed and he wished that he could be there for her. "I know."

He listened as she tried to pull herself together, but she was doing a lousy job of it.

"I'd better go now," she said, sniffing.

"Are you sure? I'm a good listener."

"Nah." She sniffed again. "I've already said too much. Where's Ms. St. James?"

"Here."

"You're joking?"

"No. She's sitting in my living room as we speak."

"Did she talk?"

"Of course not. I'm never that lucky."

"What's your next move?" She was starting to sound more like herself again.

He glanced around to make sure that he was still alone. "I don't know. I'm pretty much playing this one by ear."

The line fell silent again.

"I don't like how this is playing out. I feel that we're walking into a den of lions with blindfolds on," she said.

"Keenan is just a punk. I'm on it."

"I don't know. I have a bad feeling about this one."

"You, too?" He exhaled. "Dossman and I believe that Keenan and his gang are just hired hands—puppets, if you will."

"You have anything to support those hunches?"

"Not a damn thing." He listened to her weary exhalation.

"Do me a favor," she finally said.

"Name it."

"Be careful."

He smiled. "That goes without saying."

"And—"

"There's more?" he asked.

"Yeah. Make sure you get Ms. St. James to talk."

"You can count on it." He hung up, and then glanced back toward the living room. The small voice of his conscience preached about doing the right thing. She was vulnerable, he knew, but he had a job to do.

Entering the living room, he groaned when he saw her holding the file he'd left on the coffee table—the file that detailed everything he'd learned about her.

She looked up, stabbing him with her glare. "Some light reading?"

"I call it working overtime."

"Oh, yeah," she said, closing the folder and tossing it back down onto the coffee table. "I forgot that Tommy and I are just another job for you." A cynical smile curved her lips.

Max locked gazes with her and took a swig of his beer before responding, "I'm a cop, Kennedy. And, believe it or not, I'm on your side. I thought I proved that much tonight when I saved your life."

She looked away. "Maybe," she said, and then took a swig of her own beer. "Maybe."

He walked over to the La-Z-Boy and dropped his

weight into the seat. "I'd say that I was the least of your problems. Wouldn't you?"

Kennedy took another sip of beer and thought about Keenan, Tommy, her job, her classes, and had to admit she had little room on her list of troubles.

"Have you heard anything more about your partner?" She wanted to change the subject, plus she was genuinely concerned.

He nodded. "Actually, that call was from our Lieutenant. She says he's awake now and the doctors believe he's going to pull through."

That was a load off her shoulders. Kennedy sat on the edge of the leather couch, continued to nurse her beer. "You're trying to figure me out," she stated.

"What gave me away?" His lips gave a small hint of a smile.

"Your eyes," she answered honestly. She could feel herself relaxing under the influence of alcohol.

"Damn," he said, but didn't look sorry at all.

She smiled. "Half the time I don't know whether to take you seriously or not. You have a habit of coming off like a professional comic."

"Ah." His smile became disarming. "Let me give you a hint."

When he leaned forward in his chair, she followed his lead.

"Always take me seriously."

A strange, yet familiar yearning fluttered in the pit of her stomach, and a sudden haze clouded her head. She frowned, uncertain whether it was the beer or the intriguing man that affected her. She had a sinking feeling that it was the man.

"You want another one?" he asked.

Kennedy looked up, confused. "What?"

"Drink." He pointed to her empty bottle. "You want another drink?"

She blinked. When had she finished it? "Sure."

Max got up and went into the kitchen. As he walked away, she took her time assessing him. His gait was confident, graceful, and he didn't have a bad butt, either.

Her smile widened.

Moments later when he returned, she took in his direct profile. She looked at his shoulders and remembered their comfort. His chest had been rock hard and his abdomen was like a chiseled six-pack.

"You must work out a lot," she said, accepting the bottle he offered.

Max cocked his head. "Were you checking me out?"

Heat blazed up her neck and scorched her cheeks. "I . . . uh . . ."

He nodded, then winked. "Yeah. You were checking me out. How did I score?"

Belatedly, she shrugged and tried to lie convincingly. "Maybe a six."

"Tough crowd." He laughed and returned to his seat.

Her embarrassment lingered as she watched him blatantly assess her.

"I think I'll give you a nine. I'm not so hard to please."

She took a deep gulp from the uncapped bottle. A low rumble of laughter met her ears.

"It sure doesn't take much to embarrass you," he noted.

She shifted.

"What's the matter? Surely you've had plenty of guys tell you that you're beautiful."

She shrugged but said nothing.

He cocked his head again. "No?"

"I suppose so."

"You suppose so?" He shook his head. "Go figure. A beautiful woman who doesn't know she's beautiful. Hats off to you. You're a rare one, Kennedy."

"Thanks." She laughed. "I think."

They fell silent again, but she could still feel his gaze.

"What is it now?"

"Just thinking," he said.

"About what?"

"About when was the last time I had a woman here—at this time of night—wearing my clothes."

Her eyes narrowed. "Are you flirting with me?"

"Only if you're not offended."

She laughed, probably a bit too loud. "Oh, you're good."

"You think so?"

Kennedy nodded. "Tell me." She leaned forward and he followed suit. "Is seducing me part of the job—overtime maybe?"

Hurt stabbed his expression, as he answered in a clipped voice, "No."

She straightened. "It never hurts to ask."

"Is that right? Okay then, let me ask *you* something."

Warning bells chimed in her head. "Shoot."

"Would you like me to seduce you?"

Twenty

Kennedy didn't respond. In fact she practically forgot how to breathe as she drowned in the liquid pools of Max's eyes. Sensations spread through her body, each wondrous in their own right.

"Excuse me?" Had she heard him right?

Max's eyes never left hers. "I asked if you wanted to be seduced. I'm only asking because you've been acting odd ever since you've arrived here."

"I have not," she denied indignantly.

"No? Who was jumpy when I mentioned being shown to the bedroom? You've been blushing excessively, not to mention, gawking at my butt."

Color drained from her face. How did he know she'd been staring at him? A wave of humiliation wiped out the wondrous sensations. Had she subconsciously given him mixed signals throughout the evening? She looked at the bottle she was holding. Or couldn't she handle her alcohol?

"I'm sorry," she said, placing the half-empty bottle on the coffee table. "Maybe it's time for me to go to bed."

His gaze finally deserted hers and, for a brief moment, she could have sworn that she'd read disappointment in his eyes.

"Aren't you going to answer my question?"

His intense gaze returned to her.

Yearning bloomed, confusing her even more. It would be all right to admit a mild attraction, the small voice in her head encouraged. What was the big deal? He was a man and she was a woman.

"It's a ridiculous question," she said instead.

"Of course it is." He winked, and then took another swig of beer.

Unable to shake the feeling of being the butt of some untold joke, Kennedy crossed her arms and asked her own question. "What would you have said if my answer was yes?"

"Race you to the bedroom." He winked again, his face exploding in a smile.

She laughed, mainly because it seemed like the right thing to do. When she leaned over to retrieve her beer, her gaze returned to the manila folder that held the details of her life.

"Find anything interesting?"

Max followed her gaze. "As a matter of fact, yes."

"Oh? Like what?"

He shrugged. "Like, you've experienced quite a bit of tragedy for someone your age."

It was her turn to shrug and rely on a quote her grandmother had often said. "What doesn't kill us makes us stronger."

"No one could accuse you of not being a strong woman. Especially after everything that you've been through in the past week."

Even through the alcohol-induced haze, she knew what he was trying to do. "Yeah. I've been harassed by the police and then caught in the middle of a police shoot out at a baseball game."

"An interesting spin on events."

"It's the way I see them."

His leveled gaze seemed to evaluate her. "Sure you do."

She shrugged her shoulders and didn't say anything further.

"What helped you to cope?"

Kennedy's gaze fell and a familiar sadness embraced her like an old friend. "My son." She nodded in remembrance. "He's all I have left. He's my will to live, to be the best person I can be. I don't expect you to understand. You don't have children."

When she looked up again, she was surprised to find that Max's gaze was no longer on her. He seemed to be transfixed by something beyond her. Impulsive, she glanced in that direction, but nothing was there.

"I have a son." His voice broke.

She was sure that her expression showed her surprise.

The butterfly smile he gave her looked pained. In fact, his entire demeanor had changed.

"I even had the house with the white picket-fence, a wife, and a dog." He tilted up his bottle and drained the remaining contents in one long gulp. "So don't think you've cornered the market on pain and loss."

Kennedy blinked, surprised he'd allowed his mask to crumble before her. As she stared at him, she clearly saw his vulnerability as well as his strengths, and they both unnerved her.

The alcohol gave her courage to ask, "What happened?"

He remained quiet for so long, she thought he wasn't going to reply.

"She broke my heart," he finally responded.

Raw pain dripped from his words and seemed to

infect the air. When his gaze returned to hers it was as if they both stood naked before one another.

"Did you love Lee Carsey?" he asked.

"With all my heart," she responded without hesitation.

He nodded. "It's good to have loved, isn't it?"

"Yeah," she said in a broken whisper. It was good to have experienced love, she reaffirmed. It was the one thing that could make you glow like the sun and that would allow you to hope, dream, and embrace everything that life had to offer. Yet, at the same time, it completely terrified you: terrified you to lay it all on the line with the possibility of coming up empty . . . like she had.

"I don't think I could do it again," she said, numbly.

"Why is that?"

"It takes too much of you. Hurts too much when—"

"When it's snatched away," he finished for her.

Their eyes met, plunging them into a deeper level of intimacy.

"What about you?" she asked. "Are you willing to risk it all for love again one day?"

He frowned as he thought about it. "I don't know. If you had asked me a year ago, I would have said no. Better yet, hell no."

She smiled. "So you're a romantic?"

He shook his head. "More like an optimist. Who knows, maybe my partner is rubbing off on me. He's constantly telling me there's someone for everyone. I think he's the romantic."

"An optimistic cop. That sounds like a contradiction to me."

Max's deep laugh proved contagious, and helped erase the remaining tension that lay between them.

"You know, our sons are approximately the same age. Little Frankie is five."

"Frankie?"

"Franklin Dwayne Collier, II. We named him after my grandfather."

Max's pride in his son was clear. She draped the extra large pajama top more securely over her legs as she pulled them from the floor and tucked them beneath her. "You have a good relationship with him?"

"As close as one weekend a month will allow."

She shook her head and waited for him to return to the subject.

"My wife." He caught himself. "Make that my ex-wife. She decided that she loved someone else after seven years of marriage." His gaze trapped hers. "That someone, of course, was my best friend."

His gaze captured hers.

Sympathy was the last thing he needed, she realized, but she couldn't keep the emotion from showing in her expression.

"Hell, I don't even know why I'm telling you all of this," he said, his voice a mixture of wonder and regret.

She thought about it for a moment, and then smiled. "Maybe we're becoming friends."

He nodded and smiled, too. "Maybe we are."

Twenty-one

After their talk, Kennedy lay awake for a long while in Max's bed, staring up at the ceiling—alone. She had nervously made calls to area hospitals, and then some that weren't so local to make sure neither Tommy nor the Warners had been admitted following the trouble at the ballpark.

When she came up empty, she felt reassured that they were safely on their way, but she wasn't sure enough about it to sleep.

How easy it would be to walk up to Max and confess the past week's events. It was what she wanted to do, but something in her gut told her to hold her only bargaining chip for just a little longer—long enough to get Tommy safely out of the line of fire.

As she thought back on their discussion, she was amazed by how much they had in common, yet at the same time how different they were. She shook her head. She wasn't making any sense.

Closing her eyes, she tried to will herself to sleep, but to no avail. Instead, a pair of rich dark eyes stared at her from behind her lids. She smiled at the kindness and honesty. Slowly, her mind crystallized every detail of Max's face.

Who could ever have been crazy enough to break

that man's heart? From what she knew of him, he was a strong, caring, and funny man. She had a feeling that when he loved someone, he gave his all . . . expected the same in return.

For some reason, she tried to conjure a picture of what Little Frankie would look like—despite the fact that she had never seen a picture of the boy or his mother. The result, of course, was a tiny replica of Max.

The image thrilled her.

Kennedy's eyes flew open. *What on Earth am I doing?* She sat up and glanced around the dark room, assuring herself that no one had seen her smiling and hugging the pillow like some crazed teenager.

It was one thing to be attracted to Max. Heck, she couldn't think of a single woman who wouldn't be, but it was something else entirely to be dreaming about the man's child.

Maybe Wanda was right. All she needed was to get laid. And hadn't he offered?

Kennedy cradled her face in her hands as she tried desperately to pull her mind out of the gutter. Maybe she had sustained a head injury during the chaos at the stadium. At least that would explain her strange reaction to Maxwell Collier.

If not, it only meant one thing: she was horny.

Grabbing a pillow, she buried her face in it to stifle her scream of frustration.

Max frowned toward the hallway, when he heard Kennedy toss and turn during the night. It wasn't surprising she couldn't sleep after the day's harrowing events. After they'd talked, he did feel like he'd come away with a better understanding of her.

There were times when he felt that she, too, had loosened up toward him; maybe she had begun to trust him a little. But she still wouldn't come clean about what she knew about Underwood's death.

What he hadn't planned on was telling her so much about himself. Strange thing was that he wasn't sorry about it.

Visions of her walking around his apartment, wearing nothing more than his pajama top, drifted through his mind. He'd never seen a sexier woman. The few times when he'd caught a glimpse of an exposed leg or shoulder, when the large top shifted awkwardly, a primal urge seared through him.

She'd confessed she'd loved Lee Carsey and something within him wondered what it would be like to be loved by her. Would she give as much as she took? Would her love strengthen her man? Would she be faithful?

Something told him that the answer to all his questions was a resounding yes.

In the distance, he heard the bedsprings creak and knew that she was tossing again. Maybe he should knock on the door and see if there was something he could do to help her get some sleep.

He groaned. Who was he trying to kid? Sleep was the last thing he wanted to do, and who could blame him? The woman was every man's fantasy, and she didn't even know it.

He pressed the small light button on his watch. It was a quarter to five in the morning, and he was nowhere near falling asleep.

The bed creaked again.

He groaned again. *Will she go to sleep already?* The torture of knowing her supple body lay enveloped in *his* clothes and in *his* bed was killing him.

Max sat up. His gaze darted around the living room and then toward the long hallway.

Another creak.

He swore under his breath and went to the kitchen. Within seconds, he had a cool bottle of water, which he pressed against his temple. Maybe it *was* a bad idea to keep her here. The woman was playing havoc with his self-control.

"Mind if I have one?"

He turned and saw the object of his desire illuminated by a sliver of moonlight. The pajama top exposed a bit of her shoulder and her hair looked like she had just awakened from a night of making passionate love.

"I hope you don't mind me joining you, I couldn't sleep."

Max's body tensed and he knew he needed to shut the refrigerator door, before the light revealed his growing erection.

"Sure." He grabbed the last bottle and slammed the door.

Kennedy accepted the bottle he handed to her, but she didn't move away. "How about you?"

He blinked, uncertain whether he had missed something.

"What about me?"

"Could you sleep?"

Her voice seemed lower, huskier than normal, and Max could feel that his erection was at full mast. "No." He surprised himself by answering honestly.

She didn't say anything else. In fact, Max sensed that she waited for him to say or ask her something. But his mind couldn't stay out of the gutter long enough to think of any appropriate thing to say.

"I'm scared," she finally said. "I'm scared of what will come with the sunrise."

He knew she was referring to her son, and his heart immediately went out to her. "Where did you send Tommy?"

She turned away from the door.

Max concluded that he'd asked the wrong question.

Kennedy moved into the living room and stood by the window. "I can't talk about that now."

"All right." He shrugged. "What *do* you want to talk about?"

When she didn't say anything, he moved to stand behind her. "Unless you don't want to talk."

"I don't." She turned and lifted her face to kiss him.

Max abandoned reason as he dipped his head to receive her kiss. He had never experienced a kiss like this. The woman's lips were as soft as rose petals and tasted sweeter than wine. He pulled her closer, believing he could develop an addiction to everything about her.

Kennedy thought she could happily remain in his arms forever. It had been so long since she had enjoyed the splendor of a man's touch. She twined her arms around his neck and allowed herself to sink further into his embrace.

In one quick swoop, Max swept Kennedy up into his arms and carried her down the hallway toward the bedroom.

The next thing she knew, she felt the firm mattress beneath her while his strong body hovered above her. She drowned in the passion of their kiss, and she didn't care. She couldn't think about tomorrow and what it may bring. In this time, and in this space, Detective Maxwell Collier embodied all she ever wanted in a man, in life, and in love.

Zone Five
Saturday, 8 A.M.

Lt. Kelly Scardino watched Capt. Stephen Vincent scratch his head as he reread the report in front of him. Judging by the deeply grooved lines creasing his face, she felt safe to say that he wasn't happy.

When he finished, his steel gray eyes stabbed hers. If she were able to get out of there with her butt intact, it would be nothing shy of a miracle.

"Do you know what this is?"

"Yes, sir. It's my official report."

"No. This is killing my ulcers. That's what this is." He tossed the report aside. "I can't take that to my superiors or the press. I can't tell them that yes, my men were involved in a public shoot-out where four civilians and one cop were wounded, but no arrests were made."

"One gunman was killed, sir."

His gaze narrowed. "I stand corrected."

"It's all I have, sir."

"And I'm telling you it's not enough. What are we doing to locate this Keenan Lawrence character?"

"We have an APB out on him, but I have to tell you I think the chances of us finding him are slim to none. Since he's the leader of The Skulls, I'm sure he can make himself invisible if he wants."

"So, are you suggesting that I tell the people of Atlanta that we are unable to protect them due to the fact that there is an invisible man in our midst?"

Scardino bit her lower lip and counted to ten before she answered. "No, sir."

"I want this man found. Do I make myself clear?"

"Yes, sir."

"Good. Now where is this Ms. St. James?"

"She was released late last night."

It was his turn to count to ten. When he finally spoke, his voice still quaked with anger. "And tell me why we released her again?"

"There was nothing to charge her with."

"But she was the target, correct?"

"We suspect that she was the target. According to her statement, she was an innocent bystander."

Vincent pinched the bridge of his nose. "This day isn't happening."

She shared his wish. "We have our best people on the case. The moment we turn up something, you can be assured that you will be the first to know."

He nodded, but she knew he still wasn't happy.

"And where are we on the Underwood case?"

Just when she thought that she was going to make a clean getaway, Scardino felt the beginnings of a migraine. "Unfortunately, sir, we seem to be batting 0-2."

"A baseball joke." His smile tightened. "You're a regular riot aren't you?"

"No, sir."

He simply stared at her. "I need results, Scardino. The press is hanging me out to dry on these cases. The Mayor reminds me constantly that election time is right around the corner. And I don't mind telling you that if I go down, I'm taking you with me. Are we clear on that?"

"Yes, sir," Scardino responded.

"Good. I expect to hear from you by this time Wednesday with some real progress. Hopefully you'll have this Lawrence character in custody."

She stood, relieved that she would, after all, be able to escape. "We'll do our best, sir."

He gave her a look that demanded that they do better than that.

Scardino made her exit without a backward glance. When she closed the door behind her, her shoulders immediately drooped and her migraine spread like a forest fire.

Aaliyah arrived at the Underwood estate clueless as to what she was going to say to get an interview with Judge Hickman. Though the two women had never met, Hickman's no-nonsense reputation preceded her. Stepping out of the car, she self-consciously smoothed her pantsuit with her hands, and stared up at the beautiful colonial house.

"Come on, girl. You can do this," she reaffirmed under her breath. But doubts still managed to ebb their way into her thoughts.

She walked slowly toward the door, her mind racing for an angle that would get her past the front door.

A strong gust of wind rustled the surrounding trees and, in the distance, she heard the sound of passing cars. Another sound drifted on the wind and she stopped to listen.

Voices.

Aaliyah cocked her head. It was a man and a woman. Their angry tones pricked her curiosity. Her impromptu interview with Judge Hickman was quickly forgotten as she crept toward the side of the house to hear more.

Twenty-two

Grady Hospital
Saturday, 10:30 A.M.

The medication that dripped through Dossman's IV had him drifting in and out of consciousness. He swore that nothing compared to hospital drugs.

"Hey, you."

Dossman rolled his head to the side. A lazy smile slid into place when he saw Kelly. "Hey, yourself."

"How are they treating you in here." She pulled a vacant chair closer to the bed, and then laced her fingers with his.

He licked his parched lips. "Are you kidding? Meals served in bed, drugs, and sponge baths—I may never go home."

She laughed. "You're terrible."

"True, but don't tell anybody," he said, enjoying the feel of her hand. He suddenly wished that they were waking up together at his apartment. He longed to see her usually coiled hair spread across his pillows, or to feel her body beneath his.

"You're having dirty thoughts again." Kelly waved a finger at him. "I can always tell by that glossy look in your eyes."

"No, I wasn't." He tried to look pained by the accusation.

"No?"

"No. They were romantic thoughts. There is a difference."

Her laugh deepened. "Not with you there isn't."

"Good point."

For a brief moment, they simply stared at each other. Each read volumes of love and understanding in the other's eyes, but neither knew if their love had what it would take to bridge the troubles of age, race, or careers.

"Have you seen the doctor this morning?" she asked.

"Yeah. He said everything was looking good and, if I was a good boy, I could be out of here in no time."

"That's good to hear. I'm glad that one of us had a good morning."

"Ah, I take it that you've already spoken with the captain?"

"If I remember correctly, I believe that he did most of the talking."

"Figures."

"I can't say that I really blame him for chewing a chunk out of my butt on this one."

"Really? A chunk? Stand up and let me see."

She slapped his arm playfully. "Focus, will you?"

"Sorry. Any luck locating Lawrence?"

"Not yet. I swear if it wasn't for bad luck, I would have no luck at all."

"Well, maybe I *do* need to stop hanging out with you. Your bad luck is starting to rub off on me."

She rewarded him with another slap on the arm.

"I was just kidding."

"Sure you were." She smiled. "Anyway, I spoke to your partner last night."

"Oh? Did he happen to say why he's been such a slacker on the visits?"

"Yeah. He seems to have his hands full with Ms. St. James. She's more or less hiding out at his place."

"You're kidding me."

"No. And for some reason, I didn't tell the captain that. Maybe it's because I have a feeling he would have blown his top."

Dossman shook his head as his smile widened. "Are you sure she's just hiding out?"

"What do you mean?"

"I mean, I've seen those two together. And I would give anything to be a fly on the wall over there right about now."

Kennedy smiled at the feel of the sun's warm rays caressing her face. A rich, heavenly scent tickled her nose, further inducing her to remain drifting somewhere between dreams and consciousness, yet something tugged at her. There was something she needed to be doing.

She stretched lazily, and then froze when her legs bumped against something. Instantly, her eyes flew open, while her heart seemed to implode in her chest.

What did I do? She searched her mind for answers, but the effort only caused a loud thumping at her temples.

Max moaned in his sleep and his arm shifted to lay across her waist.

She tensed, unsure of what to do. Prayer seemed like the only logical answer. Various scenarios played in her head. In all of them, she portrayed the shameless harlot who had thrown herself at a valiant knight.

How was she going to face him?

She groaned as she grabbed her pillow and plopped it over her face to hide her shame. But her voice echoed in her ears and the pillow might as well have been a ton of bricks as far as she was concerned. How had she gotten such a severe hangover? It wasn't like she had tossed down shots of Tequila.

The phone rang and interrupted Kennedy's panic attack.

Max sat up on his side of the bed and reached over her to answer it before the second ring.

"Yeah."

Trapped beneath the weight of his body, Kennedy had no choice but to wait where she was until Max got off the phone.

"Uh-huh. Uh-huh. Uh-huh. I don't think that's a good idea. Uh-huh."

Kennedy swallowed and wished that he would hurry and get off the phone. Finally, he shifted his weight and she was immediately able to breathe easier, but it slowed considerably when he swung his intense gaze in her direction.

"She's safe," he said into the phone. "Trust me."

Though he wasn't talking to her, both statements pulled at her. She did feel safe, strange as that seemed. And there was something about the look in his eyes that pleaded with her to trust him.

They stared at each other, the phone nearly forgotten. Then the person on the other line said something that drew his attention and he turned his head. The spell was broken.

She blinked and tried to clear the haze that clouded her head.

"All right. I'll stop by the office after I see Doss-man. Uh-huh. Later." He hung up and then rolled onto his side. "I hope I didn't crush you."

"It's a great time to ask." Kennedy sat up and swung her legs over the side of the bed. A quick glance over her rumpled top told her she had at least remained clothed.

"Hey." He touched her arm. "You're not mad at me for something, are you?"

She shook her head and refused to look back at him.

"Well, you could have fooled me." He waited a moment, and then added, "It isn't about last night, is it?"

Humiliation burned through her. "You must think the worst of me."

He laughed, unaware that in doing so, he made things worse.

"I have to use the phone," she said, changing the subject. "Do you mind giving me some privacy?" It was all she could do not to start crying.

He didn't respond.

"Please?" she added.

"Not until you look at me."

His tone left no room for debate, but she did so anyway. "Please, go." Her whispered plea tumbled from trembling lips.

For a long while, the room grew loud with silence.

"As you wish."

The bed creaked as he got up. There was another rush of relief when she saw that he still wore his pajama pants.

"Just remember," he said, when he reached the door and turned back to face her. "It's almost noon."

She frowned.

"You promised to come clean then."

Had he slept with her to get a confession? Her gaze fell to the floor as that thought sickened her.

"I really need to make this phone call now."

He studied her, then said, "Fine. But afterwards, we talk. And I won't be put off so easily next time." Without waiting for a response, he slipped out of the room.

She stared at the closed door and tried to piece together exactly what just happened, but she let it go. She had more important things to contend with at the moment.

Her first call was to the Warners and she couldn't prevent the ball of alarm from rolling over her fragile emotions.

Like before, she reached the answering machine and she hung up. When she dialed her grandmother's, her hands shook and her mouth went dry. But after the seventh ring, she started to hang up.

"Hello."

The sound of her grandmother's voice temporarily rendered her speechless.

"Hello," she repeated.

"Grandma, it's me, Kennedy."

"Thank heavens. Your friends and I have been trying to reach you all night." A rush of relief echoed in her voice.

"Reverend Warner is still there?" she asked.

"No, he and his wife dropped Tommy off and left about an hour ago. But there's this other young fella here who said that he came to see you. Do you want to talk with him?"

Before she had the chance to answer, a new voice came over the phone line.

"Hello, Kennedy. I've been looking all over the place for you."

Disbelief racked her body when she recognized the deep sinister voice of Keenan Lawrence.

Twenty-three

Max slammed pots and pans around more out of frustration than in any genuine effort to cook breakfast. By the time he'd taken the bacon and eggs out the fridge, he'd started wondering why he was fixing breakfast instead of lunch. He cursed and put everything back.

Frustrated, he glanced over his shoulder, down the long hallway. The look she'd given him at the door had seemed loaded with regret and disgust. The word disgust echoed in his mind and fed his anger.

She was the one who'd come on to him. Yet, she looked at him as though he'd slipped something into her drink and taken advantage of her. He cursed again and vowed to detach himself emotionally from this situation. The only problem with that vow—he genuinely liked Kennedy St. James.

He snatched open the cabinets and searched for something to cook. His thoughts however, remained focused on the woman in his bedroom. The same woman who had felt so soft and right in his arms last night . . . The one he could have made love to but hadn't . . .

* * *

"None of this was supposed to happen," Sandra Hickman said. She jabbed her finger at the man in front of her.

Aaliyah crept closer to try to get a better look.

"It was unavoidable. He was going to the Feds with this," the man said.

"No. He would never do that to me." Sandra's voice filled with rage.

"Well, he did it. I know for a fact that he'd contacted the FBI. What does that tell you?"

"That tells me you're making this up. Marion isn't here to defend himself against your accusations."

"Sandy, Sandy, Sandy." He encircled her in his arms. "I've never lied to you. You know that. We had a problem and I handled it. All I need for you to do is to ride the wave. If everybody plays their cards right, the police will have no choice but to conclude Underwood's death as a gang related crime."

Aaliyah's eyes widened. She couldn't believe what she was hearing. Judge Hickman was involved in her ex-husband's death?

"Get away from me," Sandra snapped, bolting from his arms. "How can you trust a group of thugs to keep quiet about something like this?"

"Let's just say, I've worked with these people before. But if I ever do feel like they can't keep quiet, I will handle that as well."

Aaliyah shifted her weight, trying to see who Judge Hickman was talking to, but when she did, the bush shook.

"What was that?" the stranger said.

"What was what?"

"You didn't hear it?"

Aaliyah held her breath and prayed for a good gust

of wind to rustle the leaves again, or anything that would draw the guy's the attention somewhere else.

As if on cue, the wind picked up.

"It's only the wind," Sandra concluded; then she rubbed her head. "I can't believe this is happening. You killed my husband, Steve."

Steve. Now Aaliyah at least had a name.

"I had no choice." The man glanced back toward the bushes. "Are you sure we're alone?"

"Yes, damn it."

"Let's walk down toward the gazebo. I'll feel safer down there."

Aaliyah watched as Judge Hickman followed the man down a path that led deeper into the estate, and incidentally out of her view. It didn't matter. She'd find out who the man was before she left today. All she had to do was wait for the man to leave.

She smiled and couldn't believe her luck. Retracing her steps, Aaliyah worked her way quietly back to her car. With any luck, she would even get his picture with the camera she kept stashed in the trunk.

"I think we need to meet again, don't you, Ms. St. James?"

Kennedy's hand tightened on the receiver. "Where's my son?"

"Hey, don't worry. I'm an excellent babysitter. But you're just going to have to trust me on that. I don't have any references."

Her heart squeezed as panic shook her vocal cords. "Please, don't harm my baby."

"Now that will depend on you, won't it?"

"What do you want?"

"That's a silly question. I want you, of course. I

have to admit that I was surprised to find out that you weren't traveling with your son, but this will still work out all right. Little Tommy here can still bring you to me. Can't he?"

"Look, I'll do whatever you want. Just don't hurt my son."

"That was just what I was hoping you would say. Since there is some heat on me right now back in Atlanta, why don't you come here. How long will it take for you to get to Memphis?"

She hesitated. She'd spent all the money that she had yesterday. "I'm not sure."

"Don't even think about telling the police about this. I would hate for something to happen to the little man here."

"Please."

"Ah, I love it when women beg. But that's another thing entirely. You have until 3 P.M. Monday to get here. That should give you plenty of time. Meanwhile, I think that I'm going to just hang out here with Tommy and your granny."

Kennedy lowered her head into the palms of her hands. Grief overpowered her. There was no doubt in Kennedy's mind that Keenan planned to kill her. However, there was a chance that she could save Tommy and her grandmother.

"Are you still there?" Keenan asked.

"Yes." She sniffed as tears trickled from her eyes.

"Good. I'll see you Monday."

The line went dead.

She continued to hold the receiver, wishing like hell that she were in the middle of some bad dream. What was she going to do now?

She jumped when loud beeps told her that if she would like to make a call she should please hang up

and dial again. What had happened to the Warners?
How had Keenan found Tommy?

What did it matter? Kennedy tossed up her hands.
She had to figure out a way to get her hands on some
money in order to get to Memphis. She could try to
get a loan from Bennie. Of course the chance of pigs
flying had better odds.

She paced the floor, but she couldn't seem to churn
out a solution to her problem.

There was a crash outside of the bedroom. Max.
She'd forgotten about him. She headed toward the
door, but froze when her hand landed on the doorknob.

No police. Kennedy shook her head. What was she
going to do about the promise she'd made to Max?
Well, it really wasn't a promise, but she had the feeling that he would say otherwise. But what could she
do?

She leaned her head against the door and she
could hear the racket Max made in the kitchen.
Maybe he was creating another of his culinary masterpieces. The thought made her smile.

He was a wonderful guy, regardless of what may
have happened between them last night. She let her
smile fade again and turned away from the door.

Kelly paced the floor in front of Dossman's bed as
they reviewed the Underwood case. "The problem is
that we don't have any hard evidence that links the
Skulls to the crime."

"Right. But we do know that Keenan Lawrence
wants Ms. St. James dead for some reason. It's a good
thing that she's with Max. Right now, she's our ace

in the hole," Dossman said, pushing himself up in bed.

"Should you be doing that?"

"Probably not. But it's starting to feel like my butt is sticking to the sheets."

She shook her head as she rushed to his bedside to help. "Careful, don't overexert yourself."

Dossman took her by surprise when he tugged her down onto the bed.

She squealed, and then looked embarrassed for having done so.

He laughed against her ear and inhaled the floral scent of her hair.

Kelly slapped his arm away and pulled back to her feet. "Will you please behave? Someone from the precinct could walk in at any moment."

"Hey, what happened to my pity party we were throwing last night?"

"It ended. Your choice, remember?"

"Doesn't mean that I can't tease you with what you'll be missing."

She continued to laugh. "I'm starting to think that you also suffered some head trauma last night."

"You'd like that, wouldn't you?"

"It would probably be an improvement."

He laughed. He couldn't remember the last time they had just played with each other. For the past few months, everything had been so serious between them. Their light banter was a welcome reprieve.

For a long while, they just stared at each other and smiled.

"Assure me that we're doing the right thing by breaking up," Kelly said, taking his hand.

"I can't." His smile faded. "I'm not too sure myself."

***

"What on Earth is taking her so long?" Max wondered, looking at his watch. He'd left Kennedy well over an hour ago. "Five more minutes. After that I'm going in to get her," he decided.

Leaning over the stove, he tasted his homemade Alfredo sauce and smiled. He anticipated her surprise when she learned that he really did know how to cook. He smiled at the thought.

He took his time preparing the table. He even thought about calling the hospital, but then remembered that Kennedy was still on the phone.

Five minutes passed and he negotiated with his inner voice to give her another five. Pretty soon an additional twenty minutes had gone by and his irritation had begun to turn to worry about her.

Quietly, he walked down the hallway. He didn't hear her on the phone. In fact he didn't hear her at all. Had she gone back to sleep?

He knocked. "Kennedy?" He frowned when there was no answer. Undoubtedly, she was still mad at him.

"Kennedy, wake up." He knocked again.

No response.

He turned the doorknob and opened the door. "Kennedy?" He poked his head through the crack. His frown deepened when he saw the rumpled bed. It was empty.

He swung the door open. The room was empty. He stormed over to the closed bathroom door and knocked. "Kennedy?"

No response.

He opened the door. It was empty. Not only that,

he didn't see her clothes that had been folded on the bathroom counter earlier.

Turning, he surveyed the room again. This time he noticed the discarded flannel pajama top she had worn. It was lying beneath the open window.

Twenty-four

Aaliyah was staked out across the street from the Underwood estate with camera in hand. Adrenaline raced through her veins and accelerated her heartbeat. She was moments away from a story of a lifetime.

As she waited, visions of being a guest star on the *Larry King Live* show danced in her head.

Time ticked on at a snail's pace. And it was minutes still before she remembered that there hadn't been another car parked in the driveway when she arrived.

She frowned, and then suspected that the unknown visitor had parked in Underwood's garage. Why hadn't she thought to check the garage? She shook her head and answered her own question. She couldn't chance being caught. Lord only knew what they would have done to her. Her mind continued to reel over the wealth of information she'd learned. Her excitement waned at the realization that she was still missing a large piece of the puzzle. What had Underwood known about his ex-wife and this stranger?

"Most likely it's a crime of passion," she mumbled, and then shook her head when she remembered what the man had said. *Underwood had contacted the FBI.* She pondered that for a moment. She needed to get her hands on whatever information Underwood had found. But how?

A sleek, black Mercedes rolled down the driveway. Aaliyah readied her camera to snap a picture of the driver.

She snapped a picture, but the car's tinted windows were rolled up.

"Damn." She slung the camera into the passenger seat and started the car. She didn't come this far to lose her story now.

Aaliyah pulled her car out into traffic and followed the Mercedes.

FBI agent Jonathan Mason had done his share of tough interrogations. He even had earned himself quite a reputation for being one of the best. But he never entertained the thought that one day he would have to question his mother.

"Sorry to keep you waiting," he said, entering the small room.

DA Judith Mason looked up with a weak smile. "Think nothing of it." She waited until he sat down before continuing, "I have to admit, I'm a little curious of what this is all about."

He tossed a thin manila folder onto the wooden table top between them. "I'm following up on a case. Sort of."

"Sort of?" She crossed her arms. "Care to expound on that?"

"Well." He leaned forward and braided his fingers. "Eight days ago I got a strange phone call from the most unlikely person. He told me that he was in trouble and didn't know who else to call." Jon studied his mother.

"Go on," she encouraged.

He shrugged. "He also said that he had stumbled onto some information that the Bureau would be interested in. Putting my personal feelings for the guy aside, I listened. But he said that he needed more time. He wanted to get some more information together before coming in to see me. So he scheduled an appointment to come in and talk. Problem is, he never made it to that appointment. According to the autopsy report, he was murdered just hours after calling me."

"Underwood?" she questioned.

Jon nodded. "One and the same."

"Information on who—about what?"

"That's what I was hoping you could fill in."

"Me? What makes you think that Marion would confide in me?"

"Same reason he wanted to confide in me. He was desperate."

Judith leaned back in her chair and released a loud sigh. "I wish I could be of assistance, but I haven't a clue of what Underwood was talking about, or what he was involved in."

"Have you found anything strange in his office records since his passing?"

"Nothing. And trust me I looked."

"Why is that?"

Judith laughed. "We *are* talking about Marion, right?"

He conceded her point. "Well, it looks like I may never know what Underwood stumbled onto."

Kennedy sat near the back of the bus and fidgeted nervously. She couldn't help but stare at every black male who got on or off the bus for wondering if any of them were one of Keenan's men. She had no illusions of how much power the gang leader wielded.

She needed a plan, she realized, but doubted that she would be able to come up with one that would guarantee that she and her son would both get out alive. She needed more time to think things through. The problem was that she had no leverage. She had nothing her opponent wanted or needed, while he held everything that was dear to her.

Maybe she shouldn't have been so quick to leave Det. Collier—Max—out of the picture. She could definitely use some help. Her thoughts lingered on Max for a moment longer. She couldn't defeat the wave of guilt that crashed down on her. She'd used him, plain and simple. What was even more terrible about it was she would do it all again if given the chance.

She remembered the kiss they had shared in his living room. She had sensed a real tenderness from him then, and had felt a strong chemistry between them.

She shook her head. She couldn't think about that now. Right now she needed to figure out a way to sweet talk Bennie for an advance.

After she'd arrived at her stop, she walked quickly to the diner and used her key to the back door.

"What the hell are you doing here today?"

Kennedy jumped at the sound of Bennie's booming voice. She pivoted with one hand covering her heart. "You scared the living daylights out of me," she scolded.

"Whatever," Bennie said, walking past her. "I have a million things to do."

She followed him. "I need to talk to you about something important."

"I can't imagine what could've brought you in here on the weekend." He looked at her suspiciously. "If it's about requesting any more vacation time, the answer is no. I'm working with a skeleton crew as it is."

"No, it's not that. I—I—"

"Spit it out. I don't have all day."

"I need an advance."

His gaze jerked as if she'd announced that she carried his child.

"A what?"

"Come on, Bennie. You know I wouldn't ask if I didn't really need it."

He gave his head a hard shake. "You know the rules. If I gave you an advance, then everyone else will expect for me to do the same for them." He shook his head again. "I'm running a restaurant, not a bank."

Disappointment squeezed her heart. "I don't have anyone else I can ask. Please."

Bennie frowned. "Are you in some kind of trouble?"

Kennedy thought about lying to him, but knew the truth would probably help her get the advance. "Trouble is a mild word for it."

He studied her.

"You know I'm good for it." *If I survive,* she wanted to add.

He still said nothing.

"No one will ever know," she continued.

"Now that's what I needed to hear. How much are we talking about?"

Relieved, she wrapped her arms around him. "Thank you so much. I can't tell you how much this means to me."

"Yeah, yeah. Let's hold off on the celebration until I hear how much you need."

"Two hundred should be enough."

He gave her a worried look, then nodded. "All right." He went to get the money from the safe. When he came back he asked, "Is that all I can do for you?"

She waited until he handed her the money. Then she said, "Well, I could use a ride to the bus station."

Max's powerful punch left a large hole in the bedroom wall. How could he have been so stupid? Had this been her plan all along? Of course it was. And if he hadn't been so enthralled by the delectable Ms. St. James, he would have seen this coming a mile off.

He pivoted around the room looking for a clue as to where she might have gone. Didn't she know what kind of danger she was in? She obviously didn't know how much power Lawrence carried on the streets. After yesterday's attack, she had to know that she wouldn't last a day out there on her own.

Max rushed to his closet and shoved on the first garments his hands touched. He had to find Kennedy before Lawrence did.

Before he headed for the door, he went over to the phone beside the bed. He should call Scardino and report the latest development. His shoulders slumped at the thought. She wouldn't be thrilled by the news.

Exasperated by the realization that he really didn't have a choice, he snatched up the phone, and then froze. Instead of dialing his lieutenant's cell phone number, he hit redial.

Twenty-five

Max cursed as he slammed the phone down. The line had remained busy for the last ten minutes. He needed to know the last number dialed. He called the operator. In seconds he had the number.

"Operator, what region does area code 901 belong to?"

She paused for a moment before responding. "I'm sorry, but you will have to call information for that, sir."

"Okay, thank you." He hung up and dialed 411 and asked the same question.

"I'm showing that's Tennessee, sir."

"Tennessee? Uh, thank you." He hung up and rushed into the living room to retrieve the manila folder. Hadn't he read something about a relative in Tennessee?

Max scanned the contents until he found what he was looking for. "Jackpot. Grandmother: Alice Louise St. James resides in Memphis, Tennessee. I should have guessed that was where she would stash her kid." He closed the folder and took it with him when he rushed out of the apartment.

Once in the car, he tried the number again on his cell phone. The line remained busy. Was Kennedy now on her way to Memphis, or had she just sneaked out as a way to avoid telling him what she knew? He shook his head. If she'd wanted to hide out in Memphis, she would have left with Tommy.

Unless Tommy hadn't reached his destination.

Max cursed. Why hadn't he thought of that? He tried calling her grandmother again. A ball of anxiety churned in his gut when a recording informed him that all circuits were busy and to try his call later.

Tommy watched the tall stranger who claimed to be a friend of his mommy's. He didn't like him. The man also made his great-grandmother nervous. He could tell by the way her lips wouldn't quite turn up all the way when she smiled.

Keenan. He thought about the name. Funny. He didn't remember his mother ever mentioning anyone by that name. Tommy eyed the stranger suspiciously, in the living room with the phone tucked under his chin. How long was he going to stay here anyway?

His great-grandmother leaned over and patted his hand. They shared another nervous smile.

"Mommy told me she couldn't come here with me," he said, looking up into her kind face.

"That's what she told me, too," she responded.

"So, why is she coming now?"

"I don't know, baby." She cast an irritated look at their visitor. "Are you sure you've never met that man before?"

Tommy nodded.

Her nervousness seemed to increase. "I don't understand any of this," she whispered.

He had a feeling that she was talking more to herself than to him, but he agreed with her all the same.

"Can we call Mommy and ask her?"

"If that man ever gets off my phone. And he better not be running up my phone bill with long distance," she added angrily.

"Will you ask him to leave?"

She faced Tommy again. "I most certainly will."

Keenan hung up, and then came to join them in the dining room. His smile was wide, but unnerving. "Ah, how's the little reunion going on in here?"

"Young man, I don't know what's going on around here, but I don't like it. I don't know you and I'm almost certain you are no friend of my granddaughter's. I want you to leave my house."

Tommy's heart raced as he looked back and forth between the two grown-ups. The room grew quiet—too quiet. The strange part was that Keenan never stopped smiling.

"I'm sorry that you feel that way, Granny. I really am. I was kind of hoping that we could all get along."

"I'm not your granny, young man. And I want you to leave."

He shook his head and frowned. "Now that I can't do." He reached inside his pocket and pulled out a gun.

Bennie didn't take Kennedy directly to the bus station. First he gave her a ride back to her apartment.

"Thanks, I really appreciate this," she said as she reached for the car door handle.

He placed a hand against her shoulder gently.

She stopped and looked back at him.

"Are you going to be all right?" he asked, his voice filled with concern. "I'm worried about you," he added when she didn't respond.

"Don't be. It's nothing I can't handle," she lied. She was amazed by the note of conviction she heard in her own voice.

He smiled. "You're the toughest person I've ever met. But that doesn't mean you don't need help every once in a while."

His sincerity touched her heart. She covered his hand with her own. "Thanks. I'll remember that." She squeezed his hand, and then turned and got out of the car.

Bennie rolled down the car window. "I'll be right out here waiting for you," he called out.

She nodded, and then dashed inside her building. With her mind set on grabbing only a few things, she almost didn't see Wanda as the woman hobbled down the stairs. "There you are," Wanda exclaimed, jabbing her hand against her hip. "I was beginning to think you'd dropped off the face of the Earth. Where have you been?"

Kennedy shook her head as she continued up the steps. "You wouldn't believe me if I told you."

"Try me," Wanda said, tailing her.

The last thing Kennedy wanted to do was get her friend involved in this crazy situation. "Not right now, girl. Maybe one day, when I can look back and laugh, I'll tell you." Which didn't seem likely, she realized.

"That bad, huh?"

"Worse."

"In that case, I'll forgive you for not being here last night to meet Dr. Ward."

Incredulous, Kennedy faced her. "You brought him here?"

"Of course. I told you I wanted you to meet him."

"You're too much," Kennedy said, sliding her key into the lock. She frowned when she twisted the knob and the door wouldn't move. Had she just locked it? She shook her head, because that would mean the door had been unlocked.

"What's wrong?"

Kennedy turned the key again, and then pushed open the door. Her eyes widened at the level of destruction.

"Hot damn," Wanda exclaimed.

Kennedy crossed the threshold, but Wanda quickly reached out to restrain her. "Don't you think that maybe we should call the police first?"

Dread penetrated her bones at the thought of Max responding to the call. "That won't be necessary."

"What?" Wanda stared at her in disbelief.

Unable to offer an explanation, she simply said, "Trust me." She turned and cautiously moved further into the apartment.

Furniture had been smashed, the TV screen had been reduced to shards of glass, and the words *You're Mine* had been spray-painted in red across the living room walls.

Wanda shrank from the door. "I don't like the looks of this."

"Ditto," Kennedy whispered as she moved toward the hallway.

"Where are you going?" Wanda nearly shouted. "Someone may still be here."

Kennedy froze. She hadn't thought about that. "Well, wait right here."

"You've got to be kidding."

"Please?" she asked, with her patience nearing its end.

"All right, but I'm warning you, if you scream, or if I hear gunshots, I'm going to sprint a new Olympic record out of here."

"Just make sure you call for help when you get to where you're going."

"Deal."

Kennedy took a deep breath and returned her attention to the hallway. As she evaluated the odds of someone waiting in some darkened corner, she had second thoughts about going through with her plan.

"Will you hurry up? This waiting is killing me," Wanda said.

"I'm going. I'm going." She took another deep breath and proceeded. As she walked, broken picture frames crunched beneath her feet and the air seemed thicker.

When she opened the door to her bedroom, she feared her pounding heart would crack a rib at any moment. Tears burned at the back of her eyes as a renewed sense of violation washed over her. Everything was destroyed.

"Are you all right back there?" Wanda called out in a quivering voice.

Kennedy failed to swallow the lump that had formed in her throat, so her answer sounded like a strangled sob. "Y-yes. I'm fine. I'll be up there in a sec." She pushed past the room's clutter, deciding that it was best to focus on what was happening to her and her family.

She went to the overturned nightstand and placed the phone back on the hook. The red message light flashed and she pushed PLAY.

"Hello, Kennedy." Reverend Warner's familiar voice came out of the machine. "I'm calling you from just outside Memphis. We dropped Tommy off safely at your grandmother's this morning. We're now heading off to St. Louis. I hope we will get a chance to talk as soon as we get back. I'll talk to you soon."

She sighed in relief. At least she knew now that no harm had come to the Warners.

She raced over to the closet and jerked it open, not surprised to find the same chaos as the rest of the house. She dug around until she found her small tote bag, and then stuffed whatever clothing she could find into it. A quick dash into the bathroom revealed a shattered mirror and strewn toiletries. Again, she sucked in her horror and grabbed what she needed before heading up front.

Wanda visibly relaxed when Kennedy emerged from the dark hallway.

"I'm all set," Kennedy announced.

"Where are you going?"

She wanted to kick herself. Of course Wanda would wonder that, and she couldn't risk telling her. "I'm just going out of town for a couple days."

Wanda set her balled hands on her hips. "All right. Out with it. What's going on? And don't say 'nothing.' I'm not blind, you know." One hand swept out to indicate the apartment's condition.

Kennedy paused to contemplate how much she should divulge. She knew her friend would be safer if she kept her mouth shut.

"You're not going to tell me, are you?" Wanda crossed her arms.

"I can't."

The two friends simply stared at each other. A strange, awkward silence enveloped them.

A car horn blared in the distance.

"I better go. Bennie's giving me a ride to the bus station, and I can't keep him waiting."

"Are you coming back?"

Kennedy felt a pang of regret as she forced a reassuring smile and lied. "Of course, I am."

Twenty-six

Max's car screeched to a halt outside Kennedy's apartment. He jumped out of the driver's seat just as a car backfired in the distance. Startled by the sound, he looked up and caught a glimpse of an older model, blue Buick Regal. Out of habit, he took note of the license plate before the car disappeared from view.

He took the stairs to Kennedy's apartment two at a time. He stopped short of knocking when he noticed the door stood slightly ajar. He automatically reached for his weapon.

"Damn, you guys are quick," a woman said. "Don't worry there's nobody in there."

Max pivoted in the direction of the voice and saw a heavyset woman struggling with a pair of crutches as she descended the staircase.

"Ma'am?"

Her eyes narrowed on him. "You're a cop, aren't you?"

His hand moved away from his gun. "Yes ma'am." He reached for his badge instead.

She held up a hand. "Save it. I can't tell a fake badge from the real deal. But you definitely look like a cop." She continued to struggle down the stairs.

Max rushed over to help. "Here, let me."

"My, aren't you a strong one? I tell you, these stairs are going to be the death of me yet."

He smiled, but wasn't quite sure of what to make of the woman.

"You must have already been in the neighborhood. I swear, it hasn't been but a few minutes since I called," she continued.

He frowned. "I'm not quite sure I follow you," he said.

"Aren't you responding to my call to the police?"

Max shook his head, hating to disappoint her.

She pulled away from him. "Then why *are* you here?"

He glanced over to Kennedy's door. "Let's just say, I'm here to check on a friend."

The woman's earlier friendly demeanor vanished. "Kennedy doesn't have many friends, and certainly none that look like you. Trust me, I would know."

Max smiled at the woman's ability to pay him a compliment while calling him a liar. "We just met recently."

She crossed her arms and gave him a look of disbelief. "Where?"

"Here."

"She invited you here? Not likely."

He was impressed by the woman's interrogation skills. "No. My partner and I weren't invited. We came to question her about an incident."

"What incident?"

"I'm sorry. I didn't catch your name Mrs. . . . ."

She studied him for a moment before responding. "Mrs. Overton, Wanda Overton."

He tilted his head. "It's nice to meet you Mrs. Overton. Now, what's this about a call to the station?"

"A friend, huh?" she asked, ignoring his question. Max nodded.

Wanda's lips twitched into a half smile. "You better not be lying." With some difficulty, she moved toward Kennedy's door and pushed it open.

No further explanation was needed as Max's eyes widened at the destruction that lay before him. His hand instinctively returned to his weapon.

"There's no need for that. I told you. Nobody is in there."

"When did you discover this?"

"Actually, I was just here with her when she came home—"

"She?"

Wanda stared at him as if he had grown another head. "Yeah. She—Kennedy."

"*She* was here today?"

"Yeah, *she* was." Wanda shook her head as if saddened by the fact that he didn't seem too bright.

"Where is Kennedy now?" he demanded.

Wanda flinched.

"I'm sorry." He extracted the impatience from his tone. "Do you know where she is now?"

"No." She shook her head. "She wouldn't tell me where she was going. She just rushed in and stuffed a gym bag with some clothes and left with Bennie."

"Who's Bennie?"

The look Wanda gave him said that she no longer believed that he was a friend of Kennedy's. Max clenched his teeth. He was tired of playing Mr. Congeniality, but he gave it one more try. "Please tell me. I believe her life is in danger."

Wanda's mask of disbelief shattered before his eyes.

"B-Bennie is her boss at the Georgia Diner. They just left a little while ago. If you hurry maybe you can catch them. He drives a big old blue Buick Regal. I watched Kennedy leave from my window upstairs."

* * *

The city passed in a blur as Kennedy stared out the passenger window. Her heart ached at every glimpse of a familiar building. She couldn't help pondering the possibility that this might be the last time she saw her hometown.

As she reflected on her short life, she really couldn't say that if she had the opportunity she would have done anything differently—except she would have avoided taking the trail into the woods last week. Other than that, she really had enjoyed a good life. She was blessed to have had loving parents. They may not have had much, but they had always given the best of themselves. She had been lucky enough to have experienced love with Lee Carsey, and from that love she'd borne a wonderful child. All she had ever wanted was to be happy, and she had achieved that. She smiled at the passing cars. When it came down to it, she had had a wonderful life.

"Are you sure you're not going to need anything else?" Bennie's concerned voice invaded her private thoughts.

She needed a miracle, but refrained from saying as much. "No. I should be fine." Kennedy turned her smile to him, marveling at the ease of deception.

"Now, you're sure that you'll be back to work by next Monday?"

She nodded, then returned her gaze to the window. "I really appreciate you doing this for me."

"Don't mention it. That's what friends are for."

An image of Max flashed in her head and her smile faded. Her betrayal sat like rocks in the bottom of her stomach. Though her actions were nothing compared to those of his ex-wife, she wondered if he would judge her as harshly.

Max turned up the volume of his car radio, waiting anxiously for a response to the All Points Bulletin he'd placed on Bennie's car. He'd called his contact down at the DMV to verify Bennie's tag number. Now all he had to do was wait. He was all but certain that Kennedy's destination was Memphis; he just didn't know how she intended to get there. Had this Bennie agreed to take her? If so, which route would he take, I-20 through Birmingham or I-75 toward Nashville? One thing was clear; Max had to reach her before she left his jurisdiction.

Through the fog of troubled thoughts, his brain registered the shrill ring of his cell phone. "Yeah."

"Maxwell?"

A frown immediately creased his face at the hauntingly familiar voice.

"Maxwell?" she questioned again in a hurried whisper.

"Make it quick, Aaliyah."

"We need to meet." Her voice dipped lower.

His frown deepened. "I'm busy."

"Please. I'm onto something I know you'll be interested in."

"I highly doubt it."

Max caught the make of Bennie's car being reported over the police radio.

"I have to go now." He disconnected the call and picked up his radio's hand unit. "Please repeat the sighting for tag number 543 TYD."

* * *

As Bennie rolled his car to a stop at a red light, he emitted a gasp of disbelief at the sight of a swarm of blue and white lights flashing at him from every direction. "What in the hell?"

Frightened, he couldn't seem to force his limbs to move when a belligerent cop instructed him to step out of the car. When he finally mustered the courage to move, his body trembled as he waited for the unexpected.

Standing with his legs spread and his hands flat against the hood of his car, Bennie couldn't believe what was happening. Everything played out like a bad episode of *Cops*.

"C-can someone please tell me what this is all about?" he risked asking. Visions of being the next Rodney King made him feel sick to his stomach.

The police ignored him, but he didn't think they would be as kind if he chose to pose the question again. Behind him, he heard a car door slam just before an authoritative voice sliced through the chaotic scene.

"Where is she?"

Bennie's confusion cleared as soon as he was spun to face a towering man who had a hard gleam in his eyes.

"Where's Kennedy?"

"W-who?" Bad move, Bennie assessed, based on the angry glare he received.

"Don't play games with me, Bennie. Where did you take her?"

Torn between loyalty and fear of a beat down, Bennie simply shook his head. He had a hard time believing that Kennedy was involved in anything illegal, so he chose to remain loyal: unless, of course, a beat down seemed imminent.

The menacing cop's visible struggle with his temper kept Bennie on edge and he glanced wildly about. Were the other cops just going to let this man rough him up in broad daylight?

"Look. Ms. St. James isn't in trouble with the law. We have reasons to believe that she and her son may be in danger. Just tell us where you took her before it's too late."

"You have to do better than that, man." Bennie shook his head.

In a flash, the angry cop gripped his shirt by the collar and jerked him within an inch of his face. "She's going to die if I don't reach her before she leaves town. Is that what you want?"

This time, Bennie read the truth in the man's eyes. "No," he said, shaking his head.

"Then where did you take her?"

He took a deep breath before he took the plunge and trusted the cop. "I dropped her off at the Greyhound bus station. She's leaving on the next bus for Memphis."

Kennedy stood at the back of a long line waiting to board the bus. Once she stepped onto it, she would be nothing more than a calf being led to slaughter. But what other choice did she have?

It had been hours since she attempted to map out a plan that gave her family a chance of walking away from this alive. Perhaps somewhere in her subconscious, she had given up hope for herself.

The line moved at a snail's pace as the driver checked everyone's ticket. Aware that she wasn't in the clear yet, she continued to glance nervously about. When she reached the driver, she noticed that the older man's hands shook slightly, as though he had once suffered a stroke. But his eyes were kind and reminded her of another friendly bus driver—Leroy.

She smiled, accepted her ticket stub, and stepped onto the bus. A baby's wail was the first sound that greeted her, and she had a sudden suspicion that she was in for a long ride. As she walked down the aisle, her suspicious gaze darted to each passenger she passed.

She found a pair of vacant seats toward the back, and prayed that she'd be lucky enough to sit by herself during her voyage.

She sat down and shoved her tote bag beneath her seat just as the driver climbed onboard.

The doors jerked closed when he swung the lever.

This was it, she realized. This bus would lead her straight to her death.

Twenty-seven

The tires of Max's car squealed when he took off for the Greyhound bus station. Per his request four patrol cars followed. As they raced through traffic lights and ignored one-way signs, Max prayed they wouldn't be too late.

After years of being on the force, Max couldn't remember the last time he had feared failure. A clear snapshot of Kennedy's warm smile escalated his trepidation of the unknown and caused his foot to press even harder on the accelerator.

When the bus station finally came into view, he slammed on his brakes and caused another squeal of protest from his tires. He jumped out of the car and the smell of burned rubber assaulted his nostrils. He waved off the scent and raced into the building.

The confused crowd inside parted like the Red Sea when the police raced past them. His gaze swept the room as he headed toward the ticket counter. There was no sign of Kennedy.

"Where's the bus heading out to Memphis?" he demanded from the woman behind the counter.

She glanced toward a door and then down at her watch. "I-It just left about three minutes ago."

"Damn." He pivoted, but then turned back. "What's the bus number?"

When she gave it to him, he replied, "Thanks." He turned toward the other officers and instructed them on which bus to pursue.

The men nodded and ran back toward the main exit.

Kennedy stretched her feet out to rest on the adjoining seat. She had gotten her wish. At least she'd have a comfortable trip. She removed the fleece jacket she was wearing and bundled it into a ball so it could serve as a pillow.

She closed her eyes, enjoying the feel of the sun's warmth on her face. Her fate had been sealed. She sighed in resignation. Images of Maxwell Collier floated in her head like a dream, and she couldn't help but wonder what it would have been like if they had met under different circumstances. What would it have been like to go out on a date with him—to have the chance to get to know each other like other couples?

She smiled, imagining a romantic evening at one of Atlanta's finest restaurants, and perhaps even a jazz concert of her choice. He, of course, would have been dressed to the nines in either Armani or Versace, while she, too, would have worn a designer original. Her smile widened as her Cinderella tale continued to unfold in her head.

The bus jerked to a stop and Kennedy pitched forward onto the floor. Her right arm twisted awkwardly beneath her. Pain ripped through her as she struggled to get up.

She managed to return to her seat while clutching

her broken arm close to her body. Wincing, she glanced out of the window to see why they had stopped.

Alarm gripped her at the sight of flashing blue and white lights.

"No."

The bus doors swooshed open. She heard heavy footsteps approaching, even seconds before she saw his face.

"No," she moaned. And at that exact moment Maxwell Collier's furious gaze met hers.

"I want Lawrence found," Steve demanded into his car phone. His temper flared at an all time high. "I can't believe how sloppy he's handled everything. He may as well paint a red sign for the media, leading them to me." He listened to the man on the other line before erupting again.

"What do you mean he's disappeared? Disappeared how?"

He listened again, and wished like hell that the dim-witted gang leader stood in front of him.

"Calm down? Don't tell me to calm down. I'll calm down when that man is found. Do I make myself clear?" He glanced into his rearview mirror and frowned at seeing the same gray Honda trailing two cars behind him.

"Look, I'm going to have to call you back. Uh-huh. Later." He disconnected the call, and then adjusted the mirror. "Who in the hell is that?"

He made a sudden turn onto Tenth Street and waited for the Honda to materialize. When it did, he cursed out loud and reached over to the glove compartment for his gun.

Hands slick with perspiration, Aaliyah questioned her sanity once again. After every turn, she'd thought about bailing out of her ill thought out plan. She'd already contacted her editor promising him a story that would knock his socks off. She'd also called Reggie to tell him to meet her back at her place by seven.

However, the question of the hour was, why had she called Det. Collier? Maybe something within her wanted to make amends for the way she had treated him. Perhaps she could do that by helping him solve the Underwood murder.

She shook her head. Maybe, but it was more like she was temporarily insane. The Mercedes turned down an alley and, for the first time, she wondered where the driver was headed. Nothing was out here on this side of town.

Max towered over Kennedy. "Going on a little trip?"

She clutched her injured arm closer. "Last time I checked, it was still a free country."

His gaze grew sterner. "I need you to step off the bus, now."

"No." She watched a muscle twitch along his jawline.

"You have a choice. Either you can walk willingly or"—he removed his handcuffs from his belt—"we can give the good folks on this bus a show they'll never forget."

She glared at him and tried to decide whether to call his bluff.

His brows rose as if he could read her thoughts.

"You once said that you never knew when to take me seriously. Do you remember what my answer was?"

To always take him seriously. Seething, Kennedy stood. Her gaze fell to the crowd around her. All eyes watched her.

"Could you grab my bag? I think my arm is broken."

A spark of concern lit his eyes, and then disappeared as if she had imagined it.

"Then I guess I need to get you to a doctor."

She squeezed by him and waited for him to retrieve her things, before moving down the aisle. When she stepped off the bus, she met another crowd of curious stares. This time her audience was the men in blue.

Max descended the stairs behind her, then gripped her good arm and led her firmly toward his car.

"Are you trying to get yourself killed? Is that it?" he asked in a harsh whisper.

"I don't owe you an explanation," she hissed back.

He opened the car door for her. "We'll just see about that."

Too infuriated for a rebuttal, she got into the car and let her anger boil rampantly through her veins. She watched Max in the side mirror as he talked to his colleagues. A few minutes later, the bus pulled back into traffic and continued on its route.

Her vision blurred as she watched it disappear. What was she going to do now? Despair flooded her heart. There was nothing she could do. Everything was out of her hands.

The driver's door swung open and Maxwell slid in behind the steering wheel. She noticed the patrol cars had turned off their lights and pulled away.

"It looks like it's just you and me, kid," he said. He turned to face her.

"Lucky me."

He took in a sharp breath, held it, and then exhaled in a long weary sigh. "You do know how to try someone's patience."

"Don't beat yourself up about it. You're not doing such a bad job at it yourself."

The car fell silent for a moment. Kennedy guessed that he was calculating a different angle.

"Lawrence has your son, doesn't he?"

She turned away from him. Her actions were as much a dead giveaway as a confession would have been.

"What were you planning on doing once you got to Memphis?"

She sighed, and then gave him a sharp look. "Just cut the crap all right? I didn't have a plan. I was going to wing it."

"You were going to wing it?"

She clenched her teeth.

Max shook his head. "Funny. You look like a bright girl."

"What do you want from me? I'm trying to save my son."

"Then why won't you let me help you do that?" he thundered. "It's apparent that you can't do it alone."

"Well, *Shaft*. From where I'm sitting, it doesn't appear that you're doing such a bang-up job yourself. All you and your partner have managed to do is harass me while spewing out theories. If you were so sure who was behind all of this, why didn't you do something about it?"

His features turned to stone. "It doesn't work like that, and you damn well know it."

"Yeah. We're dealing with someone who isn't bound by the same laws and procedures you are. Why can't *you* understand that?"

He glared, but didn't answer.

Kennedy shook her head. "You can't protect me from everyone on these streets. The gangs have their own laws. I would have thought that you'd have learned that by now."

He turned from her then, his hands gripping the steering wheel, but he made no attempt to start the car.

"You know I'm right. If I'd pointed the finger at the murderer, I would have been dead inside of twenty-four hours."

"He wants you dead now. What's the difference?"

"The difference is that doing it my way might save my son."

Max leaned back against his headrest. "So, Lawrence *does* have him?"

Her lips trembled when she answered. "My son and my grandmother are in danger."

He exhaled a long, frustrated sigh. "If you do what you're planning, he's just going to kill all three of you."

She knew that, but it didn't stop a new wave of tears from spilling over her lashes. "There may be a chance—"

"There's no chance."

The profound silence that followed echoed with the crushing truth of Max's words.

"So, they're already dead then," Kennedy whispered. Devastated, she turned toward him, and he gently gathered her into his arms as her body quaked with despair.

Twenty-eight

Sandra Hickman stared into the bottom of her amber colored drink and couldn't remember how many shots she'd had. What had she done? She questioned herself repeatedly. She might as well have pulled the trigger herself that killed Marion. A deep sob tore from her.

Her beloved Marion. Dead. For little over a week, she had tried to adjust to the realization that this time their separation wasn't a result of another argument, or some knock-down, drag-out fight. He was never going to call. He was never going to walk through the front door again. And it was all because of greed, her greed for money and power.

The judicial system was going to hell in a handbasket anyway. What did it matter that she took a bribe here or there on insignificant cases?

There were more than a few cases. And they weren't always insignificant. Sandra cringed from her berating inner voice and lowered her head to rest against the bar's counter top. How many drinks would it take to shut off her conscience?

When she closed her eyes, she summoned an image of Marion from memory. She thought she'd die from the clarity her mind gave to detail. Even now, in what she knew to be a drunken stupor, she swore a trace of his favorite cologne drifted on the air.

The thought of life without him plunged her further into despair. After all, they were soulmates. More tears fell as she wished like hell that she was the one that lay six feet under at Hillandale Memorial Cemetery, instead of her husband.

He went to the FBI. She shook her head at the realization that even that betrayal didn't matter. How was it that she stood there, stupefied, when her partner-in-crime had told her he'd killed her man? It was as if he'd told her the time.

The fact was there was nothing that she could have done. Another sob was wrenched from her soul.

Sandra lifted her head. The cool waft of the air conditioner kissed her tears. Her gaze fluttered over her immaculate home, none of her material possessions filled the gaping hole in her heart where her love had resided.

You could avenge his death. Her sobs stopped and her body went still.

The idea was ludicrous. The repercussions would be severe. Regardless, Sandra warmed to the thought.

"So, you found her," Dossman said, propping himself up against a stack of pillows, though he could never quite get comfortable. "At least that's good news. Where is she now?"

"Believe it or not, she's downstairs getting a cast for her arm."

"You broke her arm?"

"No, but I could've wrung her neck for that little stunt she pulled."

"Technically, we don't have a real reason to hold her."

"Damn technicality."

Dossman laughed.

"What?"

"What do you mean 'What'? What's the real deal with you and Ms. St. James?"

Max folded his arms and thought about not answering his partner's idiotic question. "There's no deal, as you put it."

"You're in denial."

"You're a fine one to talk. What about *your* secret love affair?"

"I'm not in denial. It's just none of your business."

"And my life is an open book. Is that it?"

"It is when it involves a case."

"Is that right?" Max's expression conveyed his disbelief.

"That's my story and I'm sticking to it."

"I figured as much."

Dossman shrugged. "Frankly. I think that you two would make a charming couple."

"A charming couple?"

"Yeah. She's tough, funny, and smart. Not to mention she's extremely easy on the eyes."

"Extremely?" He unfolded his arms. "You've checked her out?"

"It's kind of hard not to. Wouldn't you say?" Dossman watched his partner sputter, and even imagined his mind churning for something clever to say. "All right, let's change the subject. I had no idea that the woman had you tongue-tied. Though I have to admit, I'm dying to know exactly what happened between you two at your apartment last night."

"I just bet you are."

"If you ever want to clear you conscience about anything at all, you know I'm here for you, don't you?"

"Cut the wise guy act. Help me figure out what our next move should be."

"Fine. Fine. Tell me the situation."

Max filled Dossman in on all that he knew and some that he speculated. When he finished, Dossman cradled his head in the palms of his hands with a look of defeat.

"It doesn't look good," he said finally.

Max stood and glanced at his watch. "Tell me something I don't know."

"I don't see where we have a choice in the matter. We have to call the FBI. Kidnapping is a federal offense."

"She's dead set against it."

"Tough. I say we play this one by the book. A child's life is in danger. It's not the time for one of us to go off playing supercop. You know what I mean?"

Max hesitated, and then nodded. His partner made sense. Though, if he was honest with himself, there *was* a part of him that wanted to play the part of the hero for Kennedy St. James.

Dossman cocked his head with a bemused grin. "Damn, you got it bad. Are you daydreaming now?"

"I thought you were supposed to change the subject."

Tommy clutched his grandmother's hand, surprised that she had managed to stop trembling whereas he could not. The man promised them that it would all be over soon, once his mother got there, but Tommy found himself praying for her not to come. The man planned to hurt her, despite his claims of being a friend.

"Does this place have a basement?" Keenan asked.

"Yes," his grandma replied, tilting her chin.

"Good. Take me to it." He waved his gun at her.

She stood and Tommy did likewise.

"What are you going to do with us?" Tommy asked boldly.

Keenan's mouth twisted into a cruel smile. "I think I'll keep that a secret, little man." He returned his gaze to the older woman. "Show me."

His Nana stiffened, and Tommy squeezed her hand for reassurance. She turned and led the way to the basement.

Keenan's smile widened at the sight of a key jutting out of the lock. "Look what we have here. It's Christmas in October. Get in."

She pulled Tommy against her. "Please don't do this."

"Don't waste my time begging. It won't do you any good." He took a threatening step forward. "Now get in there."

Their hard gazes battled before she complied and pulled Tommy in with her. The door slammed closed and impenetrable darkness surrounded them.

Tears rushed from Tommy's eyes as violent tremors shook his small body. Images of the boogeyman and other scary monsters crowded his imagination.

"Shh, baby. It's going to be all right." She lowered onto her haunches to console him.

He tried to stop trembling, but it only got worse. "I'm scared," he admitted.

Her arms enveloped him in a powerful hug as she confessed, "So am I."

* * *

"Good news. It's not broken," Kennedy said with a crooked grin. "It's just a sprain."

He returned the favor before unloading the bad news. "I've talked to my partner and we both agree that we need to go to the FBI on this one."

Her smile vanished. "No." She turned on her heel and headed toward the exit.

With lightning speed, Max blocked her from the door.

"Out of my way, Collier. You have no right to hold me. I know it and you know it."

"I don't need you here to call in the FBI, Kennedy. It's going to happen with or without you."

Kennedy's jaw clenched with anger. "If you do, he's going to kill my son. Doesn't that mean anything to you?"

"It means everything. That's why we have to do this. We have less than forty-eight hours. We don't have a choice."

She rolled her gaze from him, too angry to speak.

"If you would just be honest with yourself, you'd realize that you can't solve this on your own. Lawrence wants you because you witnessed a murder. He'll killed your son and grandmother to get to you. That is if he hasn't killed them already. We're talking about a no win situation here."

Kennedy sagged into a nearby chair. Despair descended on her like a ton of bricks.

Max knelt beside her. "I'm sorry. If I thought that there was another way—"

"Don't be sorry. You're right." She wiped her eyes dry. "If you think this is what it's going to take to save my family—then let's do it."

He took her trembling hands into his. "I know just the guy to call."

Twenty-nine

Max pushed open his door and swept out a hand to allow Kennedy to enter first.

"What's this?" Her tote bag slid to the floor at the sight of the elegant diningroom table.

"I . . . uh . . . prepared a lunch for us this afternoon, before I discovered you'd jumped ship."

She lifted a curious brow. "More soup?"

"Hardly." He moved over to the table and lifted the top off his serving dish. "Homemade Crab Alfredo. It's ice cold now."

She walked over to the table with a timid smile. "Well, for what it's worth, it looks beautiful."

He turned in her direction with a disarming smile. "Too bad you didn't stick around, this meal would have knocked your socks off."

Her heart fluttered. "I'm here now."

"So you are." His steady gaze probed hers. The room's temperature seemed to rocket and Kennedy suddenly found it hard to breathe. Her mind suddenly cluttered with memories of being locked in his arms, and relishing the taste of his lips.

She blinked and broke the hypnotic spell, only to notice that he, too, stared at her with the same level of intensity.

Kennedy cleared her throat. "Maybe this time I should fix us something to eat."

"Not only are you beautiful, but you can cook as well?"

She blushed at his casual compliment. "There are a lot of things I can do that aren't in your little folder."

"Really?" He inched closer. "Like what?"

Her thoughts scrambled and she quickly forgot what they were talking about. "Huh?"

Max laughed, jolting her out of her stupor.

"Oh . . . uh . . ." She shook her head and laughed at herself. "I must be getting tired."

"Uh-huh." His smile widened. "Why don't we cook dinner together?"

"Together?" she repeated dumbfounded.

He nodded. "Unless being with a great chef, like myself, makes you nervous."

"You know, you talk a lot of trash, Mr. Campbell's Soup."

"You're never going to let me live that down, are you?"

"Not if I can help it," she said, then realized the oddity of her comment. The chances of her returning to his apartment, or even seeing him again after all this madness, were slim to none.

"All right then. What would you like to cook?" He turned and walked to the kitchen, then stopped short when he saw the mess he'd left.

"My goodness." Kennedy joined him. "It looks like El Nino hit this place."

"I was creating."

"Please don't start that again."

He shrugged. "If you insist."

"How about we just order a pizza?"

"I don't know. It doesn't sound too romantic."

Kennedy's brows rose in curiosity. "Were you trying to romance me?" Her knees felt weak when he flashed her another potent smile.

"What if I was?"

"Why do you always answer my questions with other questions?"

Another shrug. "Didn't realize I did."

"Bull. I think you do it in order to avoid giving me a straight answer."

"Do you now?"

Her smile widened. "There you go again."

"All right. You caught me." He turned away from the kitchen.

Kennedy followed. "So, what's your answer?"

"To what?"

"You're impossible." She laughed. "I asked you whether you were trying to romance me."

"Ooh."

"Ooh," she mimicked him.

"I might have been," he finally answered.

"It's a yes or no question." She couldn't believe her eyes. He was actually blushing.

"Then the answer is yes."

Flattered, her body warmed beneath his intense gaze.

"To be honest," he continued, "I've been attracted to you since the moment I laid eyes on you at the Georgia Diner." He lifted one hand and caressed her face, marveling at its softness. "There is just something about you."

Kennedy placed her hand atop his, unsure as to why she stopped him. "I'm a woman with a lot of baggage. You don't want to get involved with me."

"I have a lot of closet space."

She shook her head. "You don't understand."

"Look, Kennedy. I'm not going to force you to do anything that you don't want to do, especially right now. But I do want you to know that I'm interested."

Spellbound by his sincerity, she gravitated toward him as if he had spoken magic words. She wasn't disappointed when his lips met hers halfway.

FBI Field Office, Atlanta, Georgia
Sunday, 8:45 A.M.

Special Agent Jonathan Mason reviewed Kennedy St. James' statement, satisfied that at least part of the Marion Underwood puzzle had been solved. Keenan Lawrence's case file had been delivered to him in less than thirty minutes, and plans to retrieve Thomas and Alice St. James were in full swing.

"Why didn't you come to us earlier?" Mason asked, returning to his desk.

"I told you. He warned me not to involve the police." She glanced over at Max, who smiled encouragingly.

"And you have had no further contact with Mr. Lawrence since this morning?"

"I've already told you, no."

Agent Mason locked gazes with her.

"Look, are you guys going to save my son or not? I've told you everything I know."

"Calm down, Ms. St. James. We're doing the best we can. I just need to get some more information."

Her shoulders drooped and she rolled her eyes heavenward. "This is a big waste of time."

He smiled. "Trust me, we are going to do all we can to protect your family. I'm only going over things because sometimes people bury things in their sub-conscious, perhaps dismissing them as irrelevant. More times than not though, it's the small things that are important."

She dispelled some of her anxiety in a long sigh. This had to have been the longest day of her life.

After another hour of questioning, Kennedy and Max were led to another room, where a dozen agents were gathered, all either on phones or hunched over mounds of paper.

"We've already contacted our Memphis office. We'll fly up within the hour to establish a liaison."

Kennedy pivoted toward the agent, her eyes wild with desperation. "What about me? You're not leaving me here are you?"

Mason set a hand on her shoulder as he responded in a soothing voice, "We wouldn't dream of it."

She then turned to Max. "You're coming, too, aren't you?"

His gaze dropped and he slowly shook his head. "This is no longer a police matter, Kennedy. I would just be in the way."

She tugged on his arm, petitioning for his full at-tention. When his gaze returned to hers, her body grew warm and the air seemed dense.

"But I need you there."

His lips fluttered at the corners before a full smile carved his mouth. "Then I'll be there."

The door swung open and a man, whom Kennedy assumed to be another agent, entered. "Is there a Detective Collier in here?"

"I'm Detective Collier," Max said, stepping forward.

"We have a call for you; a Lieutenant Scardino."

He nodded, and then turned back toward Kennedy. "I'll be right back."

She nodded and watched with a whirl of tangled emotions as he disappeared with the agent.

Max followed the immaculately dressed agent into a small room at the opposite end of the hallway, all the while wondering why his lieutenant wanted to speak with him.

"Hello."

"Collier?" Scardino's firm voice filtered through the phone line.

"Yeah?"

"I hope you're sitting down."

He took a seat. "I am now. What's up?"

"I have a new case I need for you to go and check out."

"Now? I'm still working on a few things down here."

"Ms. St. James is the FBI's problem now. I need you back here."

Max mumbled a curse under his breath.

"I think you'll be interested in this one. A homicide has been reported down on Memorial Drive. The victim has already been identified as Aaliyah Hunter."

Sandra packed bank records, receipts, and even tape recordings of every illegal transaction she had participated in into a large box. She had kept such records for insurance. Now it was time to cash in.

She then addressed the box to the one man she knew at the FBI to be trustworthy: Jonathan Mason.

Though she had never been a great fan of the Mason family, she did respect their reputation. There was a part of her that wanted to laugh at the irony of the situation, but she couldn't.

"I'm doing the right thing," she reaffirmed repeatedly. Who was she kidding? If she was honest with herself, she'd know that the right thing to do was to turn herself in. However, the thought of enduring the humiliation of a media frenzy, and doing jail time, scared her. Instead, she elected to take a different approach.

Sandra removed the .45 automatic that she'd kept on the top shelf of her walk-in closet. She loaded the gun and then secured it in the holster that fit snugly against the small of her back.

She checked her appearance in the mirror and hardly recognized the woman dressed head to toe in black, with her long hair brushed back into a ponytail. "It's time to fix this mess we got ourselves into," she said to her reflection. She turned and slid on her leather jacket, picked up the box, and left to execute her plans.

"I'm not going to be able to go with you after all," Max informed Kennedy when he returned. "I'm sorry."

"But, I need you there," she sputtered, struggling to explain again. "I don't know how much more of this I can handle alone."

"I know, but something has come up." Guilt rattled his voice as he thought back on Aaliyah's phone call. She'd called him in her time of need, and he'd practically hung up on her.

"I've been assigned another case."

Hurt shadowed her features, but she managed to nod in understanding. "I guess this is it then."

A long silence hung between them as their gazes probed one another.

"It doesn't have to be," he said.

She gave him a weak smile. "Twice you've saved my life. Thank you."

"Ah, gratitude. I was just beginning to think that the emotion was foreign to you."

Kennedy's smile slid wider as she playfully slapped at his arm. "You're not funny."

Mason suddenly appeared beside them. "We're ready to leave, Ms. St. James."

She nodded and the agent gave the couple some privacy.

"In case I didn't tell you earlier, I really do appreciate all that you've done."

"I was just doing my job . . . and it was my pleasure."

Another lapse of silence hovered over them.

"Thanks again." She stood on her tiptoes and kissed him.

Max cradled her face and prevented her from delivering just a quick peck. He dipped his tongue into her mouth and had to stop himself from moaning aloud. The world spun into a blur as the sweet intoxicating taste of her mouth urged him to hold her close.

Kennedy sank into the feel of his embrace. Her mind drifted lazily on a cloud, as the smell, the feel, the taste of him threatened to undo her.

When the kiss ended, they both still savored the residue of their passion.

"This is definitely not good-bye," he whispered.

She smiled tenderly at him. "I hope not."

"We're waiting on you, Ms. St. James."

"Of course." She returned her attention to Max. "I have to go."

"I'll be thinking of you," he said, and kissed her once again.

It was excruciating when they finally parted and he watched her walk out with the FBI agents. But he held no illusions that, somehow during this crazy case, he'd found the one thing he hadn't known he was searching for: love.

Thirty

Kennedy stared blankly out the small window while the past week replayed in her head. Eight days. Had it really been such a short time? It seemed more like eight years. Eight years of being on the run and looking over her shoulders; eight years of being scared and tired.

Agent Mason leaned over in his seat and interrupted her thoughts. "Don't worry. It will all be over soon."

She nodded, not in the mood for small talk, and wished like hell that she could turn off her frazzled emotions. "I should have called the police."

"I'm sorry. What did you say?"

Kennedy took a deep breath and closed her eyes as she exhaled. "The night of the murder. I should have called the police the first chance I had."

They sat for a moment in silence. Her words hung in the air like a death sentence before Mason attempted to ease her guilt.

"You know what they say: Hindsight is always twenty-twenty."

She looked at him, shaking her head. "I watched a man die and didn't even try to bring the murderer to justice because I didn't want to get involved. How pathetic is that?"

Mason crossed his arms and looked as if he was trying to choose his words wisely. "I've been in this business a long time, Kennedy. And I've dealt with numerous people. Most of them had the best of intentions. I believe that you are one of those people."

"Is that supposed to make me feel better?"

"It was meant to help you forgive yourself. You made a mistake. The point is that you're cooperating with the authorities now."

"But it wasn't by choice. It was the only way I could find to try to save my family."

Mason shook his head. "Look, I've never been good at this. Hunting down clues and catching bad guys are pretty much my forte. All I can tell you is that people make mistakes. Very rarely do they get the chance to correct them."

She nodded as she thought about what he said.

"Plus, there's no proof or guarantee that things would have worked out any different had you gone to the police. Keenan would still have gone after you. You would still have tried to send your son to what you thought to be a safe place, and we would still be making this trip to do our best to save them."

That scenario made sense to her. Incredibly, her guilt lifted. "I think you lied to me."

"Oh?"

"I think you're better at this than you say."

A broad smile monopolized his face. "No comment."

Max arrived at the scene of the crime, wondering if he was mentally up for this. The answer was no, especially since he couldn't keep his mind off Kennedy. Now wasn't the time to leave her alone, not when she didn't have anyone else to lean on for emotional support. She needed him, she'd said so herself. And he wished like hell he could be there for her.

He got out of the car and made his way almost to the yellow crime scene tape before he heard his name called. He turned and was surprised to see Lt. Scardino edging her way toward him.

"Glad you finally made it," she said.

"I got here as soon as I could."

She tilted her head, indicating that she wanted him to follow her. "I got a call from Hunter's editor. Seems your favorite reporter was working on the Underwood investigation."

"I know. I saw her and a cameraman at the crime scene."

"Did you share any information?"

He frowned and shook his head. "Come on. You know me better than that."

She nodded, then continued. "According to her editor, she called him this afternoon saying that she had stumbled onto a major break in the case."

This time, it was Max's turn to nod. "I know. She also called me."

"Come again?"

"It's not what you're thinking. In fact, I didn't really give her the chance to explain."

"What time was this?"

"I don't know. I guess around three o'clock."

"What did she say?"

Max struggled to remember. "Something to the effect that she had found something that I might be interested in. I told her that I highly doubted it, and that I had to go."

Scardino's frown deepened. "Sounds like you need a refresher course on human relations skills."

"I feel bad as it is, Lieutenant."

"Sorry." She took a deep breath and watched her men scurry about the crime scene. "I figure, if I'm going to get my butt chewed by the captain about this investigation, I may as well get my hands dirty. Plus for the time being, you are short a partner."

He raised a questioning brow. "Are you trying to tell me we're partners?"

"For the time being."

He smiled.

Scardino paced. "What I don't get is if Keenan Lawrence killed Underwood, and he's in Memphis, then who killed Hunter?"

Max shrugged. "It could've been one of Lawrence's gang members."

"Possible. But that doesn't really explain why a group of street thugs suddenly took it in their heads to start killing off such high-profile people."

"I don't think that they have. Underwood was a hired hit. I'm willing to bet my badge on it."

"Hired by whom?"

"Haven't a clue."

They fell silent.

Max turned and surveyed his surroundings. "What was she doing out here?" he asked in a low voice. He thought back to their phone conversation. She had called him on his cell phone. "Wait a sec." He walked back toward his car.

"What do you got?" Scardino asked, trailing him.

He opened his car door and grabbed his cell phone from the passenger seat. He reviewed the Caller ID screen. "I just want to see something. He headed over to the gray Honda and punched the button for his phone to redial the number Aaliyah had called from.

The officers searching the victim's car jumped when the car phone rang.

"She called you from the car," Scardino said, nodding.

Max disconnected the call. "What time was the body discovered?"

Scardino reviewed her notes. "We received the call at approximately seven-fifteen A.M."

Max bit his lower lip as he entertained a thought.

"What are you thinking?"

He shook his head, not sure that he wanted to share his hunch.

"Come on, *partner.* Share."

He laughed. "All right. I'm just wondering if she was tailing someone."

She frowned. "All right. Remind me not to ask you to share next time."

"It's a possibility. She calls me, frantic, telling me she's discovered something I may be interested in. What could that be? She knows that I was investigating the Underwood murder. Her editor also told us that she was working on that case. Is it so far-fetched to believe that she stumbled onto *someone* as opposed to *something?*"

"We may have something here," Detective Washington announced from the car.

Scardino and Max turned in time to see the officer lifting a camera she'd sealed in a plastic evidence bag.

"It was stuck in between the console and the passenger seat," Washington added.

"Can we be that lucky?" Scardino asked.

"If we are, it will be a first for me."

* * *

"I thought I'd find you here," Sandra said, slamming the door behind her.

Steve glanced up from his desk, and held up a finger to ask her to wait a moment while he finished his phone call. She took the opportunity to retrieve her gun from her back holster, careful not to be caught.

"No, sir. I have everything under control. Lawrence will be taken care of. Yes, sir. Yes, sir."

Sandra rolled her eyes as she waited for the call to end. She knew now who sat on the other end of the line. Don Gaetano, an infamous drug lord who had been a thorn in the side of the city of Atlanta for more than a decade.

His reign of power had enabled him to purchase all the right cops and the right judges to keep his business running smoothly, including her. Her nightmare had begun when Gaetano had asked if Underwood would also agree to join his payroll. To everyone's surprise, Marion had refused and then gone so far as to contact the FBI, which signed his death warrant.

Steve ended his call. "To what do I owe this unexpected pleasure?"

She smiled. "Actually, I'm surprised that you weren't expecting me."

He leaned back in his chair and studied her. After a moment he shrugged, as if he had concluded that she was harmless. "Now, why would I be expecting you?"

Sandra revealed her gun. "Because you killed my husband. Remember?"

"Ah," he said. He didn't flinch. "So, you've come here to kill me?"

"I have a hunch that it'll make me feel a hell of a lot better."

His expression eased into a wide smile. "And you think I'm just going to sit here and let you shoot me?"

"I don't *think* you have a choice."

"Obviously, you haven't thought this through. Maybe now is the time to do so."

"I've done all the thinking I need to. This madness needs to stop."

"This isn't the way to handle this. Come on, Sandy. I'm a pawn in this game, just like you. Killing me won't change that."

"I already told you. Killing you is just going to make me feel better. I have a little surprise for Gaetano, too. By tomorrow morning the FBI will have received some rather interesting reading."

Steve's features hardened. "You didn't."

"Oh boy, did I ever."

He shifted slightly in his seat. For the first time, she realized that she didn't have a clear view of his hands. Her gaze flew to his face. His smile now resembled a smirk.

She squeezed the trigger and was simultaneously speared with a blinding pain that stole her breath and sent her spiraling into a black vortex.

Thirty-one

FBI Field Office
Memphis, Tennessee

"When will I be able to see my son?" Kennedy asked Mason as he ushered her into the building.

"Soon," he assured her.

"And when is that exactly?"

Mason gave her a patient smile. "First, let's meet with the special agent in charge here, and hear the plan of action. Maybe your questions will be answered then."

She nodded, but a bubble of anxiety welled up within her. Questions plagued her mind. Were Tommy and her grandmother safe? Were they scared?

Upon passing through another heavy door, she was greeted by another dozen plus agents.

Mason instantly recognized one of them and thrust out his hand to receive a firm handshake. "Hagan, it's good to see you again."

The man identified as Hagan stood at least a foot taller than Mason, which in itself was impressive. He was an older man who possessed a full head of white hair and a pair of the most startling blue eyes she had ever seen. For reasons she couldn't explain, she felt more confident.

The men exchanged brief greetings before turning their full attention to Kennedy.

"And you must be Ms. St. James?"

She nodded.

"Good. Let's get started on getting your son back, shall we?"

Scardino stared blankly at Det. Dorsey, sure that she hadn't heard the officer right. "Please run that by me again."

"You haven't heard? It's all over the radio. Judge Hickman killed Captain Vincent. Their bodies were discovered in his office early this morning."

Scardino sank into her seat, grateful that she hadn't actually hit the floor. "Where is Judge Hickman now?"

"Grady Hospital. Apparently, Captain Vincent squeezed off a shot. She's listed in critical condition."

Scardino shook off her shock and dismissed the detective with a wave of her hand. "Nothing is making sense lately," she mumbled under her breath.

There was a rap at her door seconds before it burst open and Det. Washington entered. "We have those pictures developed."

"I hope there's something that we can use."

Washington handed her the folder.

Scardino's stomach lurched and threatened to return her lunch. She blinked and stared at the photo of the sleek black Mercedes pulling out of 3016 Orchard Street. She recognized the car immediately, and knew the residence just as well.

She dropped the photographs on her desk and slumped to prop her head against the palm of her head. "Could you tell Detective Collier to come in here, please."

"Yes, ma'am." Washington left her office without further ado.

Meanwhile, Scardino tried to wrap her brain around what the pictures meant. "What was the true relationship between Vincent and Hickman? And how did it relate to Aaliyah Hunter's death?

"You asked for me?" Max poked his head through her doorway.

"Yeah. Come on in."

He entered and closed the door behind himself.

"Take a seat," she instructed.

He frowned, but took a seat.

"Tell me. What do you make of these?" She slid the pictures across her desk.

He leaned over and picked up the photographs. He recognized the estate immediately, but was clueless about the black Mercedes pulling out of the drive. "Whose car is it?"

"Let me tell you this," she said, braiding her fingers together. "Captain Vincent is dead.

"His body was found this morning. That's not all. Judge Hickman seems to be our killer."

"What?"

"Now take another look at the pictures taken with Ms. Hunter's camera."

He looked again. "This is the Underwood estate."

"And that's Captain Vincent's car."

"I'm confused."

"That makes two of us. I want a search warrant for Ms. Hunter's residence as well as one for Judge Hickman's. We've got to see if there's a paper trail of any kind of payoffs."

Max stood, still shaking his head. "Do we know where Hickman is?"

"Grady. Captain Vincent managed to shoot her. That's all I know, for all the good that does us."

"You know, if we're working under the theory that Aaliyah was killed for stumbling onto something or someone regarding the Underwood murder, then it's quite possible that either Hickman or Vincent—"

Scardino held up her hand. "Please don't say it."

"Someone needs to. We're looking at quite a mess here."

Again Scardino rested her head into the palms of her hands. "We're going to be slaughtered in the media whatever way this one goes."

"Mind if I ask what your gut is telling you?"

"My gut has taken a trip down south. And my head is telling me that I should have never gotten out of bed this morning."

Kennedy's heart raced as she waited for Special Agent Hagan to alert her that all systems were go for her to call her grandmother's residence. She was so nervous, in fact, that she worried whether she would actually be able to say anything at all when Keenan picked up the phone.

She prayed constantly, and often wondered if God could hear her. She tried to seek comfort in the fact that God looked after children, but such thinking floundered under the realization that bad things happened to children every day.

Lowering her head, she found herself wishing that Max were there. He had an incredible ability to calm her. She hadn't fully realized that before. Perhaps it was only now that he wasn't there that she could realize how much she had allowed herself to come to depend on him. There was even a small part of her that realized that she'd been hoping that he was going to rescue her from herself when she'd hopped on the bus to Memphis. She had almost counted on it.

Kennedy shook her head. She wasn't making any sense. She had only known the man for about a week, and she was acting as if he had always been a part of her life. But there was no other way to describe what was between them either.

"We're ready, Ms. St. James," Agent Hagan said, picking up a pair of headphones and placing them over his ears.

She nodded and picked up the phone. While she struggled to keep her hands from trembling, she silently reviewed the questions the F.B.I. had prepared for her. Of course the only thing important to her was whether her family was still alive and well.

The phone rang and she waited patiently for her grandmother to answer. Her heartbeat started accelerating somewhere between the fourth and fifth unanswered ring. What if it was already too late?

The answering machine picked up. She glanced nervously at Agent Mason.

He nodded as a signal for her to leave a message.

At the sound of the beep, she spoke into the receiver. "Hello, Grandma. It's me—"

A loud banging sounded over the line, seconds before Keenan interrupted her. "Ah, Ms. St. James. It's so nice of you to call. I'm kind of surprised. You're a whole day early."

"What have you done with my family?" she asked, already forgetting about the FBI's questions.

"Don't worry. They're safe."

"I don't believe you. Put them on the phone." It was useless to try and control the tremor in her voice, just as it was useless to try to rein in her emotions.

"You have no other choice than to trust me," he said with a snicker.

At that, Kennedy grew combative. "Go to hell. You've got to be crazy if you think I'm going to agree to meet with you when you've probably already killed my family."

Agent Mason suddenly appeared at her side and tugged on her arm.

She ignored him and continued to lay into Keenan. "Put my son on the phone or the deal's off."

The line fell silent for a long moment, and Kennedy thought her worst fears had come true. He had already killed them.

"All right, then. I'll go get them," Keenan finally said.

Kennedy slumped against Mason as a wave of relief swept over her. The first glimmer of hope returned and began to penetrate her fear-frozen heart. But she was too terrified to fully accept that warmth before she was able to hear her son's voice.

Keenan cursed as he stormed through the house. This whole venture had turned out to be one big pain in the neck. He had kept the child and the grandmother locked in the basement now for nearly twenty-four hours, and actually had no clue as to how they fared. He didn't care. He'd planned to killed them anyway, after he'd finished his business with the kid's mother.

He turned the key to unlock the door leading to

the basement and pushed the door open. Complete darkness greeted him, but it was the room's eerie silence that unnerved him.

"What y'all doing down there?"

There was a slight rustling sound, and then two forms stepped into the dim light from the open doorway. He eyed them suspiciously, disconcerted by their strange behavior. Then he remembered why he had come—the phone.

"Send the boy up. His mother wants to talk to him."

The little boy raced out of the safety of his great-grandmother's arms and hurried up the stairs.

A lopsided grin curled Keenan's lips. He was actually looking forward to tomorrow, when he would finally get the chance to get back at Lieutenant Preston K. St. James for all the years of grief the man had given him . . . by killing the rest of his family. He loved it when he got paid to do what he wanted to do already.

With a hearty laugh, Keenan re-locked the basement door and led the boy to the phone so he could talk to his mother for the last time.

Max returned to Scardino's office, not at all pleased. "We've got a problem with the warrant."

Scardino opened her month to respond when the phone rang. "Hold on for just a sec," she said, lifting a slender finger to ask him to wait, before answering the phone. "Scardino."

He exhaled and settled into the chair across from her desk. Almost immediately his thoughts returned to Kennedy. The weight of guilt for having left her now seemed impossible to continue to bear. He wanted to be there with her . . . to be there *for* her.

He glanced at his watch. What were they doing now? Had she had a chance to speak with her son? It was the not knowing that threatened to drive him crazy.

Would she call when it was all over? He'd like to think so, but he wasn't sure. Right now, he wasn't sure about much of anything when it came to Kennedy St. James.

He did know that he'd told her the truth the other night. The depth of the feelings he felt for her surprised him. He'd become wary after going through such a disastrous marriage.

But now here he was again, feeling all those things he'd sworn off.

"All right. I'll be right over," Scardino said and hung up the phone.

Max snapped out of his reverie and locked gazes with his lieutenant.

"Well, it looks like we may not need that warrant. Judge Hickman pulled out of her coma about an hour ago, and she seems to be quite the chatter box." She stood and reached for her jacket.

He stood as well. "She made a confession?"

"According to Detective Evans she has."

"Well, what did she say?"

"Only that Captain Vincent ordered the hit on her husband."

"Ex-husband."

"Whatever." She moved from behind her desk. "Evans said that Vincent came to her house yesterday and confessed."

"Ms. Hunter's photos."

"Exactly."

Max looked at his watch, his mind again returning to Kennedy.

Scardino stopped and stared at Max, watching as a frown creased his features. "Are you all right?" she asked, moving next to him.

"What?" he blinked, then looked contrite for having been caught with his mind wandering.

She offered him a knowing smile.

"Yeah, of course. You want me to come to the hospital with you?"

"I'm not sure that will be necessary." She studied him some more. "You know Mike told me that you have grown fond of Ms. St. James. Until now, I thought that he was just joking around. You know how he can get."

Max nodded.

"But he's right, isn't he?"

A denial sat at the tip of his tongue, but he thought about how she had opened up to him the other night regarding Dossman, and he thought better of it. "I'm worried about her, and her family."

"And?"

Max knew that she was asking as a friend and not as his boss. For a moment, it seemed odd for them to exchange roles so casually.

"I care for her," he admitted finally, then added as an afterthought, "a lot."

She nodded. "You know, I had thought to send Detectives Randall and Hendricks to Memphis."

Max folded his arms and continued to nod as if unaffected by her decision to send other officers to ensure the extradition of Keenan Lawrence. Of course, that was if he was caught.

"I'm thinking that perhaps you should be the one to go," she said.

Their gazes met. "I can handle things here. Maybe even have Detectives Randall and Hendricks sub until you get back."

"Are you sure?" His heart skipped a beat.

"I'm positive. Detective Washington can go with you."

Max resisted the urge to pull Scardino into a fierce hug, but he was powerless to stop the broad smile that spread across his face. "Thanks. You have no idea what this means to me."

Scardino opened her office door with a wistful smile. "Don't be too sure of that," she said.

Thirty-two

Alice St. James tugged, pulled, and shoved boxes as thick clouds of dust rose from nowhere and everywhere at the same time and sent both her and Tommy into coughing fits.

"What are we doing," Tommy asked. Glancing over his shoulder toward where he knew the door to be, though it was too dark to see it. "He might come back if we're too loud," he warned in a small voice.

"Don't you worry about him none. We've got a little surprise for him." She swept her foot across the floor.

Tommy coughed as another wave of dust floated around him. "What's that?" he asked.

"That's grandma's secret." She reached down and pulled open the latch she'd found by touch and memory. "You see, years ago your great-grandfather had this wonderful idea of how we'd survive if we were ever in a nuclear war. Actually, that was a great concern for a lot of people back in the fifties and early sixties. So he decided to build this great fallout shelter."

"And we're going to hide in there?"

"No. We're going to leave the house this way. You see, the shelter also serves as a tunnel out of the basement. There's a passage that will take us all the way to the wooden shed that's down by the pond."

Tommy clutched his grandmother's hand. "The bad man won't be able to get us?"

"That's right."

Tommy moved into her arms and she gave him a fierce hug and a quick peck.

"Now let's hurry up and get out of here." She carefully felt her way up the stairs to the door and lowered the two wooden bars that barricaded it from the inside. "This should give us a little more time," she whispered, then turned back down to lead her great-grandson to safety.

FBI Field office
Memphis, Tennessee

Kennedy threw her arms around Max, surprised by the wave of relief that overwhelmed her the moment she saw him. "I can't believe you came."

"You said that you needed me." He folded his arms around her. "How are you holding up?"

"Lousy. It seems to be the theme of my life lately." She gave a laugh that was nearly a sob. "That bastard has them locked in the basement."

"Is he working by himself?" Max asked, astonished.

She pulled out of his embrace and wiped at her tears. "As far as we can tell—yes."

Max's expression showed confusion. "Sounds a bit unusual for a gang leader, don't you think?"

She shrugged. "I suppose so. I haven't really given it much thought. Agent Mason says it should make it easier to rescue Tommy and Nana." She studied Max's troubled expression. "What are you thinking?"

"Actually, I wondering if this kidnapping is more like a vendetta or something."

"With me?"

Max shrugged it off. "Maybe not. I don't know. Something just seems fishy about this whole thing."

Kennedy lowered her gaze. The memory of her talk with Keenan in the park surfaced. Hadn't he mentioned her father? "Maybe you're on to something there."

Their gazes met again.

"My father spent a lot time pursuing Keenan and his gang in the latter part of his career. I'd say it wasn't far from the point of obsession."

Max nodded, clearly deep in thought. "So maybe, just maybe, this has become more than just an opportunity to eliminate a witness to the Underwood murder for Keenan. He could, quite possibly, still be trying to win some kind of war with your dad. What better way is there to do that than to destroy the man's family?"

"Okay, we have our mobile unit in place," Agent Hagan informed them.

Kennedy nodded, knowing he referred to a surveillance vehicle disguised as a telephone company van. "How close are they to the house?" she asked. Her grandmother's property was a good seven acres.

Hagan moved over to the table where a detailed map of the area was spread out. "The closest pole is here, which is approximately thirty to forty feet from your grandmother's property line."

"How about sneaking onto the property down here?" Mason asked, pointing to the wooded area by the pond.

"We're already on that. Our second unit should be ready within the next few minutes."

"Are you going with them?" Max and Kennedy asked in unison.

"Yes," Mason answered.

"I'm coming with you," Kennedy announced.

"There is no way I can authorize that," Hagan said.

"I'm going, either with or without you," she informed him with her chin lifted in determination.

Hagan matched her expression. "You'll be tampering with a federal investigation. I strongly advise that you reconsider."

Kennedy lowered her gaze and hoped that her look of contrition appeared genuine but, secretly, she still had every intention to follow.

"You'll have to get up earlier if you plan to fool me," Hagan admonished.

Kennedy abandoned her submissive act and once again met his direct gaze. "I'm going."

The four-member circle grew silent, despite the intensity of the battle of wills between Hagan and Kennedy.

"You promise to stay out of the way?" Hagan asked, finally.

"Scout's honor." She held up one hand in the scout's gesture.

Hagan's eyes narrowed. "I don't remember reading anything about you being a Girl Scout."

Kennedy let her hand fall. "Don't get so technical."

That finally won a smile from him, as well as his agreement. "All right. You can come."

Kennedy smiled triumphantly.

"You just make sure that you stay out of the way."

She looped one arm through Max's. "I promise that you won't even know that we're there."

* * *

Keenan jerked open the refrigerator and peered inside to see if there was anything in there worth drinking. "Milk, orange juice, cranberry juice." He shook his head and slammed the door. What he wouldn't give for a beer right now.

Bored, he headed back into the living room. When he passed the phone, a sly smile curled his lips. He was willing to bet that Kennedy had never expected for him to out-smart her. He puffed out his chest with pride. He was actually going to pull this off.

Of course, he'd probably fallen out of Captain Vincent's good graces, but he was confident that could be remedied. His smile broadened as he continued to move toward the window.

Before he reached it, something nagged at him—something about the telephone call between Kennedy and her son. What was wrong about that phone call?

There was always the chance that she *had* gone to the police, he thought.

Keenan shook his head, sure she wouldn't risk her son's life that way. She knew what he was capable of.

But that didn't necessarily mean that she wouldn't try to call his bluff.

He turned and rushed back to the phone. He dialed star sixty-nine and was disappointed when the automatic operator informed him that the last call couldn't be traced.

He struggled to rein in the wild possibilities running through his head. Slamming the phone down, he tried to calm down. "So, the number is untraceable, no big deal," he said to himself.

But he couldn't help thinking, what if she did go to the police? Were they on the line when she called? Were they planning something? He suddenly had an uncontrollable urge to check on his two hostages. He rushed to the basement door and turned the key, but the door wouldn't budge.

He threw his weight against the door several times before it moved at all. "I'm going to get you for this," he threatened. What in the hell had the old lady put in front of the door? he wondered wildly.

The telephone rang.

"The Feds," he mumbled under his breath. His assumption could easily be way off base, but he couldn't afford to think so. His anxiety renewed itself and he slammed into the barricaded door with more gusto.

Something cracked and then gave way. Keenan was suddenly airborne and plummeting down the flight of cement stairs. His body roared with pain while he struggled in vain to stop his fall. His head banged into something hard at the bottom of the stairs. A brilliant flash of stars danced before his eyes.

He groaned and struggled for what seemed like forever before he managed to stand. When he had succeeded, he remained so disoriented that he had to lean against a nearby wall for support.

The gun, he remembered, and looked around for it in the dim light from the doorway above. What had happened to his gun? He had holstered it before he started bashing the door, but there was no sign of it now. The phone had stopped ringing, too, he realized. He touched his head, not at all surprised to feel a thin trail of blood.

"I'm going to kill you for this," he hissed, taking a step toward the stairs and immediately regretting it. He waited a few more seconds, hoping the feeling of vertigo would pass and he'd be able to actually trust his footing.

Despite his throbbing temples, Keenan was able to

discern that he was at a disadvantage. He wouldn't put up with that for long.

As he started to move again, he kicked something and reached down. It was his gun. He smiled wickedly. The scale had just tipped back in his favor.

As he stood up again, he bumped into something hard and sharp. Why hadn't he checked the basement out more thoroughly before storing his hostages down here? he thought. The place seemed to be filled with sharp stuff. He halfway expected the old lady to jump out and attack with some rustic tool at any moment.

"Come out, come out wherever you are," he urged in a sing-song voice. When he stopped and strained to hear any signs of life, all he heard was the sound of his own labored breathing.

"I know that you're in here. You may as well come out now and make it easier on yourself." Again, he waited, listening, and still there was no response. His anger escalated and his patience snapped.

"Fine, Granny. Suit yourself. I'm going to enjoy putting a bullet in the center of your head, and the little brat, too." He laughed. "I only wish that your son were still alive to see me finally come out on top."

The silence stretched. Something was definitely wrong.

FBI's Mobile Unit

Kennedy hung up the phone. "Something's wrong. He's not answering."

"We just picked up the sound of a gunshot within the house," said the FBI agent monitoring the van's listening devices.

Kennedy covered her heart with a trembling hand as she turned toward Max. "Gunshot?"

"I don't like this. It's like we're working with blinders on." Mason said, a frown marring his features.

Hagan agreed. "Let's move in."

"Wait!" Kennedy shouted, not at all comfortable with the speed at which everything was happening. "Is that wise? I mean—"

Max moved to her side and tried to console her. "Baby, let's let them do their jobs."

Agents filed out of the van as if heading off to war.

The look in Kennedy's eyes grew wild as her emotions tumbled out of control. She wasn't prepared for this. Why were there gunshots? *Please God, don't do this to me.*

Max gathered her into his arms. "It's going to be all right."

"You don't know that," she said, twisting away. "You don't know anything."

Max flinched at her hurtful words, but accepted her rejection with an understanding heart. "You getting upset isn't going to help things," he said reassuringly.

Kennedy clamped her mouth shut and nodded in agreement with his logic. When she returned his gaze again, it was with a brave smile. "I'm glad you're here."

"Just think of me as your shelter from the storm," he answered.

Kennedy went still.

"Are you okay?" he asked, concerned.

"The shelter. Th-the fallout shelter."

Max stared at her dumbfounded.

She grabbed his arm. "There's an underground fallout shelter with a passage that leads into the house basement. I had completely forgotten about it."

Thirty-three

Tommy clutched his great-grandmother's hand as she led him farther into the dark tunnel. She'd sworn that they'd be safer down here; the problem was that he didn't feel safe. In fact he couldn't remember ever being so scared in his life. He almost preferred to face the boogeyman that lived under his bed. Surely it couldn't be as bad as this.

"Maybe we should go back," he suggested. His voice trembled as he edged closer to tears.

She didn't stop pulling him forward. "We're almost there," she said.

Hadn't she said that before? He sniffed, then with his free hand wiped his eyes dry. The last thing he wanted to admit was that he was scared—that would mean he was a fraidy cat. At least that was what Jimmy had always teased. Tommy took another worried glance over his shoulder. How could she be so sure that the bad man wasn't going to come after them?

Keenan scrambled around the basement, cursing the fact that the cramped quarters had very little lighting. But the harder he searched the angrier he got. They had to be down here somewhere. He double-checked all the windows. They were painted closed. Was there another way out of there?

His foot caught something hard and his body pitched forward, but he caught himself before landing face first on the floor.

"What in the hell?" He turned and edged back toward what appeared to be a metal rod in the middle of the floor. "What in the hell is this?" The moment he voiced the question, the answer swirled inside his head.

"No, goddamn it." He tugged on the rod only to have his suspicion confirmed. He muttered another stream of curses. How long had they been gone? Did it matter? He had to find them before it was too late.

He stared down into the dark tunnel and wondered where it led. *Well, there is only one way to find out.* Certain that he had no other alternative, he tucked away his gun and crawled down the cramped space.

Kennedy burst out of the FBI's mobile unit like a bat out of hell with Max close on her heel. When he finally caught up with her, he swung her around to face him.

"Where do you think you're going?"

"I'm going to save my son," she shouted, then tried to pull away.

He shook his head. "Come on, Kennedy. You're not thinking. If you go out there alone, the only thing you're going to do is get yourself killed."

She clamped her jaw shut and glared at him.

It took everything Max had not to shake some sense

into the woman. In fact, he had to mentally count to
ten before trying to reason with her again.

"The right thing to do is to go back in there and
have one of the agents radio for Agent Hagan and
Mason."

Kennedy jerked out of his grip, determined to do
things her way. "Fine. You call them. I'm going to
see if I can find the entrance hatch."

Agent Mason watched as Hagan and his men took
their positions around the house when out of the corner of his eye he saw Kennedy and Max running toward the woods in the opposite direction.

What is she up to now? he wondered. He took another glance at Hagan, but his curiosity returned to
the couple racing off into the woods.

Keenan pried his way through thick cobwebs while
periodically erupting into coughing fits. He may as
well have crawled into a coffin, he assessed.

He stopped and allowed his eyes to adjust to the
darkness before plunging further into the unknown.

Kennedy scrambled around the pond, desperate to
locate the entryway into the underground tunnel.
"It's got to be around here somewhere," she mumbled.

"I can't let you do this," Max said.

"Maybe it's on the other side," Kennedy said, ignoring him.

"Are you listening to me? There's a better way to
do this, Kennedy."

"Maybe you're right." She raced over to the other
side.

"What are you two doing up here?" Mason stepped from behind a small wooded area and into the clearing.

Max breathed a sigh of relief.

"There's a tunnel that leads into the basement," Kennedy said, without stopping her search. "If only I could remember where."

"Then we need to go back and tell Agent Hagan. He can get his men out here—"

"I found it." Kennedy dropped to her knees and removed a large square patch of fake grass to reveal an iron ringlet. "I can't believe it."

Max rushed over to her.

Mason followed. "Wait, we have to call for backup."

Kennedy grunted as she strained to open the latch.

Max laid his hand against her shoulder. "Baby, maybe he's right about this one."

She ignored the men and lowered herself into the dark hole.

"Damn it," Max and Mason swore in unison.

"Kennedy, wait," Max called, then scrambled down after her.

Mason struggled with what he should do, then resolved himself to following Kennedy and Max.

Kennedy moved slowly through the dark tunnel with her hands stretched out before her. With any luck, maybe she could feel her way to the basement.

"Good Lord, what is that smell?" Max asked.

"If I were you, I wouldn't ask questions you really don't want to know the answer to," Mason said as he pulled up the rear.

Kennedy smiled. "I'm happy you two decided to join me."

"That makes one of us," Max countered.

"Amen," Mason agreed.

* * *

Alice couldn't figure out how to relock the latch from inside the fall-out shelter.

"Maybe we can just stay in here." Tommy glanced around and saw shelves packed with dusty canned items. At least they had light in this room. He pivoted around again. The room was actually kind of neat.

"My great-grandpa built this thing?"

Alice smiled with pride. "He sure did."

"Wow. He must have been real smart, huh?"

She nodded and then reached down to pinch his cheek. "I think I see a little bit of him in you."

Tommy's smile widened. "Really?"

"Yes. Really."

"Cool."

"We better keep going. I can't figure out to get this latch locked," she said.

"Do we have to? It's dark out there."

"I know sweetheart, but we're not too far from the exit. We have to go call the police."

"Are they going to put the bad man in jail?" he asked with hope in his voice.

"You bet they are."

"Okay. Then let's go."

Hand in hand they started to move toward the opposite end of the shelter, but a loud screeching sound from the exit door stopped them.

Tommy jumped and hid behind his grandmother's leg while she swallowed a scream of terror.

Kennedy gave the steel door another push, and then yelped in alarm when she fell through to the other side.

"It's Mommy!" Tommy shouted, then sprinted over to his mother.

Kennedy exploded with relief. "Tommy!" Her arms opened in time to receive her son. "I'm so happy to see you."

Alice breathed a sigh of relief. "I swear, Kennedy. My old heart can't take too much more excitement."

"Are you sure about that?"

Alice, Kennedy, and Tommy jumped at the sound of Keenan's voice, their hearts pounding at the sight of his gun.

Keenan's sly smile grew confident. "Don't tell me I just stumbled onto one of those mushy family reunions."

Kennedy pushed Tommy behind her.

"I'm so happy you could join us, Kennedy. I was just beginning to think that you wouldn't be able to make it."

"Please. Let them go. I'm the one you really want."

"I'm sorry, but I can't do that," Keenan answered with a firm shake of his head. "You know, it just occurred to me that you three are the last surviving members of Lieutenant St. James's family."

"You're despicable," Alice hissed.

Keenan swung his aim in the older woman's direction. "I think I'll do you first."

"No!" Kennedy shouted, jumping to her feet.

Keenan's eyes widened as he swung the gun back in her direction and fired.

Max and Mason burst through the small portal door.

"Freeze!" they shouted in unison. Keenan, however, was unable to respond. His aim missed its mark as Kennedy hurled her small but determined body into him.

The gun flew out of Keenan's hand and landed without another discharge.

Kennedy pounded Keenan with her fist until she drew blood.

Alice raced to comfort Tommy.

Max raced over and pulled Kennedy off Keenan.

"It's a shame we had to stop her." Mason holstered his gun and handcuffed a dazed Keenan.

"Especially when she's doing such a wonderful job."

"Tell me about it."

It took Max a while to calm Kennedy down. Even after they succeeded in getting everyone back up to the surface, her body continued to quake with anger and disbelief.

A medical team arrived to check on everyone. Afterward, Hagan's men asked a series of questions.

Max never left Kennedy's side. "Are you sure you don't want to go to the hospital?"

She shook her head and clung to the warmth and the security of his body. "No. I just want you to hold me."

He obliged. "I think I can handle that," he said. As he held her, he couldn't help but wonder where they would go from here. He couldn't imagine not being involved in this courageous woman's life. He just hoped that she felt the same way.

Thirty-four

Four months later
Valentine's Day

Kennedy took one last glance in the mirror. Max was due to arrive at any moment and she planned to knock his socks off. She had borrowed and saved for the last two months to buy the sexy Versace knock-off, and was pleased with the results.

The plunging neckline was perhaps more daring than what she was used to but, what the heck, Max was worth it.

The doorbell rang.

Kennedy took a deep breath and closed her eyes. "Lord, please help me not make a fool of myself," she prayed.

"Ms. St. James?" Eve poked her head around the bedroom door. "Mr. Collier is here for you."

"Thank you." Kennedy took another look in the mirror and worried about her upswept curls. "How do I look?"

Eve's face brightened with a wide smile. "You look beautiful."

"Thanks." Kennedy walked over to the teenager and squeezed her hand. "Wish me luck."

"You won't need it."

Together the women moved from the bedroom toward the living room.

The sight that greeted Kennedy there warmed her heart.

Max knelt beside Tommy. They seemed engrossed in a man-to-man talk. She couldn't hear what they were saying, but her son wore a smile as wide as Texas and continued to nod enthusiastically as Max whispered in his ear.

Seeing the two men in her life share such an intimate moment nearly brought tears to her eyes.

Eve cleared her throat and Max looked up.

A look of astonished pleasure instantly washed over his features.

Kennedy held her breath, sure that once she breathed her spell would be broken.

"You look stunning," Max finally managed to say.

"Thank you." Her heart drummed wildly in response to his intense gaze. "You look pretty good yourself." And it was more than true. She was more accustomed to seeing him in jeans or casual wear. The polished gentleman who stood before her deserved cover model status across every magazine in America.

"You look like a Barbie doll, Momma," Tommy said in a voice filled with wonder.

"Why, thank you, sweetie."

"You're welcome. Guess what. Max brought a surprise for you."

Kennedy's gaze returned to Max. "Did he now?"

"Uh-huh. He said that I could give it to you. Do you want it?"

Her curiosity heightened. "I would love it."

Tommy rushed to the kitchen.

"Here, let me help you," Eve said, following the eager little boy.

Max laughed. "You have a wonderful son," he said, moving toward her.

Kennedy smiled. "Thanks. I think he likes you."

"I hope so."

The number of butterflies in her stomach increased the moment he slid his arm around her waist. "I don't know how long I'm going to be able to keep my hands off you," he said.

"That was the general idea."

"Should we ditch dinner and head straight to the Ritz-Carlton?"

She slapped his shoulder playfully. "I don't think so. I plan to show this dress off to everyone in Atlanta."

"That's an awful lot of men I'll have to fight off."

"Aren't I worth it?"

He laughed and stole what was meant to be a quick kiss, but the moment their lips met it turned into a long passionate interlude.

The sound of giggles interrupted them and Kennedy turned, blushing with embarrassment . . . and pleasure. When she saw what her son was holding, with Eve's help, a small gasp escaped her open mouth.

It was the most exquisite arrangement of roses, irises, and baby's breath she had ever seen.

"For me?" Kennedy asked, incredulous. Her misty gaze swung to the man beside her.

"I can't think of a woman more deserving."

She awarded him with another kiss, and swore the man made her toes curl.

"You have to read the card, Mommy."

"All right." She moved toward her son with shaky

knees. As she removed the card, it seemed that everyone waited with bated breath.

"Read it out loud," Tommy insisted.

Kennedy smiled and turned to check for a nod of approval from Max. Then, nervously, she opened the card with trembling hands. "To the most extraordinary woman I have ever had the pleasure to meet and fall in love with. Be careful with my heart. Max."

She quickly wiped at her eyes before tears ruined her makeup.

Max eased up beside her. "I take it you like them."

"They're lovely." She turned and slid easily into his embrace. Before she knew it, she was lost in his sensual gaze.

Eve cleared her throat again.

Kennedy and Max laughed at themselves.

"I guess we better go, if we're going to make our eight o'clock reservation," Max said.

Kennedy nodded and picked up her purse and shawl. After she said her goodnights, they were off to Sambuca's for an evening of dinner and music.

The moment they entered the restaurant, Kennedy was enthralled by the atmosphere and the live jazz band. As she'd expected, she had a great time. For the most part, she felt like Cinderella at the ball.

In the course of their meal, Max played with, caressed, and held her hands. In the back of her mind, she couldn't help but remember the daydream she'd enjoyed aboard the Greyhound bus, and couldn't believe that somehow it had come true.

When their meal was over, Kennedy's thoughts turned to what was to follow.

"Do you still want to go?" Max asked, as if reading her mind.

She squeezed his hand gently and nodded.

The waiter returned with the check and they were off.

Kennedy had never been to the Ritz-Carlton before. But she knew, from the moment that they stepped into the lobby, that she would never forget it.

Max opened the door to their suite and Kennedy stepped inside with a confidence she didn't feel. To her surprise a trail of rose petals led to the bed and to a table holding a bottle of champagne and some scrumptious looking hors d'oeuvres.

Beside the bed sat her tote bag. She turned and lifted an inquisitive brow.

"Wanda."

"Oh, so now you're enlisting my neighbor's help?"

Max shrugged. "It wasn't hard. When I told her what I had planned, she nearly broke her leg again jumping for joy."

Kennedy laughed. "In that case, I'm surprised that she's not here in a cheerleader's outfit rooting for me."

"I got the impression she wanted to be." He pulled Kennedy into his arms. "I figured we could manage without a cheerleading squad."

"You do, do you?"

"Mmmm-hm." He kissed her with all the promise of what was to come.

She was overwhelmed by a wave of vulnerability, but at the same time determined to experience the promises of his kiss. Her eyes remained closed in pleasure, long after he pulled away.

"I'll go get some ice for the champagne and give you a few minutes to get ready," he murmured. He kissed her again, then left the room with the ice bucket.

Max hummed to himself as his sense of anticipation

heightened. He rounded the corner and came to an abrupt halt.

"I don't believe this."

Dossman, wrapped in a pale blue, terry cloth robe, stopped shoveling ice into his bucket and looked up. "Max, what the hell are you doing here?"

"Apparently the same thing you are. Don't tell me you and Scardino—"

"Don't ask and I won't have to lie."

The men shared a smile, before Dossman asked, "You're here with Kennedy?"

"Since *my* life is an open book, the answer is yes."

"Ah, love is definitely in the air tonight. If we play our cards right, maybe we'll have a double wedding."

Max's mouth fell open. "A wedding? Am I hearing this right? You proposed?"

"More like, I'm about to propose. Wish me luck."

Max patted his back. "All right. Your creeping days are over."

"Let us hope." Dossman took a deep breath. "I'll tell you how it all turns out tomorrow."

"I'll keep my fingers crossed."

Kennedy stared at her reflection, gaping at the provocative red, lace teddy. In certain poses she looked ready to pour out of it.

Her heart skipped a beat when she heard a light rap on the door.

"This is it," she warned herself, then turned to let Max in.

Max blinked at the vision in red that greeted him at the door. His heart pounded in double time. The soft floral scent of her perfume captivated his senses and he moved toward her as if pulled by some strong magnetic force.

He reached for her, unable to suppress the urge to touch her. "I thought that this night would never arrive," he whispered against her ear.

Kennedy listened to the hypnotic rhythm of his heart. She was suddenly unsure of what she was supposed to do. It had been so long since she had done anything like this. What if she disappointed him?

He lifted her chin, then slowly allowed his fingers to trail lightly over her warm, silky cheek, stroking it soothingly. He then leaned in and kissed her again, erasing all her doubts.

She strained against him and the swollen tips of her breasts pressed against him.

He responded with a guttural groan.

Encouraged, she slid her arms around him and molded her body against his muscled frame.

Max's hand slid down her back, causing a ripple of desire to course through her.

First relieving him of his jacket and tie, Kennedy grew more aggressive with each article of clothing. When, at last, the rest of their clothing had fallen to the floor, she marveled at the sight before her. Her gaze traveled from his handsome face down to his broad chest and flat stomach, then stopped at his swollen manhood, where she carefully slid on a condom.

She pressed her naked body against him and felt her flesh tingle.

Max scooped her up in his arms and carried her to the bed. His hands seemed to be everywhere at the same time and she loved the feel of them exploring her body.

"I need you," he said in a husky voice. Then he sprinkled kisses across her stomach.

She couldn't seem to catch her breath as his mouth returned to taste every inch of her breasts before he gently parted her legs and allowed his tongue to explore the valley between her thighs.

Kennedy cried out his name at the invasion of his tongue. She gave herself over completely to the expertise of his lovemaking.

Max entered her slowly and together they discovered their own frenzied rhythm. Soon ecstasy flooded the depths of her soul, turning her body into liquid fire.

As the lovers lay breathlessly in each other's arms, Kennedy whispered, "I wish that it could always be like this between us."

"Be careful. You might just get what you wish for."

She laughed as she snuggled against him. "That's the whole point. Tonight, I've learned that dreams can come true, and I have so many dreams for us. And, look at you. You've been awarded joint custody. Your son will now live six months a year with you. Aren't you happy?"

"Thrilled." Max fondled one of her tan nipples before taking it into his mouth and making a popping sound.

Kennedy playfully pushed him away. "Will you get serious?"

"I've told you. I'm always serious."

"What about you?"

"Look, I found all I've ever wanted the moment we met. And I'm determined to keep you no matter what it takes."

His words melted the last fears in her heart, and she scattered feather-light kisses across his face before giving in again to the magic of his lovemaking.

Own the Entire ANGELA WINTERS
Arabesque Collection Today

__The Business of Love
                    1-58314-150-2 $5.99US/$7.50CAN

__Forever Promise
                    1-58314-077-8 $5.99US/$7.50CAN

__Island Promise
                    0-7860-0574-2 $5.99US/$7.50CAN

__Only You
                    0-7860-0352-9 $4.99US/$6.50CAN

__Sudden Love
                    1-58314-023-9 $4.99US/$6.50CAN

__Sweet Surrender
                    0-7860-0497-5 $4.99US/$6.50CAN

More Sizzling Romance by
Gwynne Forster